Daniel Morgan's Time

PHILIP J NORD

ARCHWAY
PUBLISHING

Archway Publishing books may be ordered through booksellers or by contacting:

Archway Publishing
1663 Liberty Drive
Bloomington, IN 47403
www.archwaypublishing.com
844-669-3957

Scripture taken from the King James Version of the Bible.

ISBN: 978-1-6657-1116-6 (sc)
ISBN: 978-1-6657-1117-3 (e)

Library of Congress Control Number: 2021916977

Print information available on the last page.

Archway Publishing rev. date: 12/13/2022

Dedicated to:

My Mother Dorothy May she rest in peace She loved
reading and passed it onto her children

PARATAXIS

(Many Stories)

There is a somewhat unique structural style of writing to Daniel Morgan's Time known as parataxis. It was first used by Herodotus, known as the father of histories. His historical document also included the cultural and societal written in fiction but true to the times. It is like a series of interrelated short stories that proceed one after the other like hanging hangers of information one after the other. Daniel Morgan's Time uses this structural style but also refrains from segway and has no chapters. It is just a series of interrelated short stories in chronological order.

CONTENTS

2525

I t is the year 2525. I'm sitting in the veranda outside of the Terrain Mall. The smell of desert wildflowers is in the air, and it is pleasant and refreshing. There was a thunder and lightning storm that stopped a few minutes ago, and the smell of ozone is in the air. My name is Dooty Grainger, and I'm the general manager of the historic holographic project. My team consists of Gaughy, who does data animation relating to people and animals, Cary (pronounced *Car E*) who also does data animation but involving inanimate objects such as trees, bushes, flowers, fences, and houses. Drapey is our historian, and Early does QA (quality assurance) and repairs such as holographic melting or disintegration and general data and image repair.

For posterity's sake and possible future generational understanding, I will describe our current science and technology as we know it today. Terrain architecture is exactly as it suggests—that is, the use of terrain to build living and working spaces. It generally has no outside walls or roofs. For this reason, it can be ecological and have flora and fauna. It can either be made on level with the terrain or have a hill-like structure. It can be built with trees and forest on top or growing from within. It can have streams or ponds inside or out. It is generally accessed through tube travel tunnels, pedestrian passages, or parking garages accessed by electromagnetic vehicles.

Tube travel is a type of transportation involving a tube tunnel with a vehicle traveling in a vacuum tube. It generally travels about one thousand kilometers per hour, but it moves slower in populated areas. It can be a single tube or a series of tubes connected like train cars. Each tube is for singles or small groups such as adults with children or families and friends. There are electromagnetic cars that are piloted automatically.

There are also space elevators. These are also tube tunnels, but they are vertical and transcend to space stations in low earth orbit. A space station is a platform held stationary in space by small electromagnetic rockets. It also travels at about one thousand kilometers per hour and can have singular tubes or many attached together.

Other technology includes self-cleaning floors, walls, and ceilings. There are air chairs and holographic imagery accessed by ring computers. Meals are served on recyclable dishes and silverware that is disposed of, melted, and reformed on location. Clothes are generally single use and disposable with the material recycled. Lavatories are designed to recycle the waste directly to soil used for farming or natural ecosystems, thereby saving the streams and rivers from pollution.

All the energy used in the system is from electromagnetic power provided by the sun's rays into the atmosphere, which is also known as *ion* or *free energy*. It is accessed by Tesla coils and transmitted through the air by Tesla transporters.

Government has changed. There are now departmental presidents elected every six years. There is a president of state, a president of the treasury, a president of defense, a president of the interior, a president of housing, a president of homeland security, and a president of transportation. The legislature and judicial branches are the same. Local communities take precedent in matters of law. A city's laws trump the county's, which trump the state's, which trump the federal government's. The only exception is constitutional law; then federal law trumps all.

Money is guaranteed. Payment is made just by walking in an establishment and having your eyes scanned. Whenever you make a purchase, you automatically take a share in that company. Housing is free. If an individual falls behind in revenue, a government guaranty kicks in—but only for normal living conditions that are already tracked.

To keep entrepreneurial motivation going, there is no limit on enterprises, and regulations are kept to a minimum. If you want better than public housing, cost is your only limitation.

Recent Physics

The infinity hypothesis is as follows:

The equation: ie = ffwfsfgremrqtmst

Whereby infinity times everything equals free
fall times weak force times strong force times gravity
times electromagnetic radiation, times quantum theory
(string theory) times mass times space times time.

This is the unification theory, and it is also known as the theory of everything theory. The big bang theory proposed that the universe collapsed into a singularity where the time before thirteen billion years ago is thought of as being nothing. The theory stated that the universe would collapse as expansion slowed and then reverse itself. In the late twentieth century, a Nobel Prize–winning scientist showed that the universe was actually accelerating, thus conclusively debunking the big bang theory.

Free fall creates energy. Free-fall catalysts help form forces; namely, strong force, weak force, gravitational force, and electromagnetic force as subatomic particles coalesce and cause attraction and repulsion.

Free fall trajects that matter can convert to energy and vice versa as string vibration that is chaotic due to free fall. Space and time provide for free fall. Free fall propels cosmic energy to quasar-clumped fractal matter into an emulsion that is seemingly an entire universe in human understanding but is actually, in cosmic terms, about the size of a point on the end of a pin and getting infinitely smaller while the universe expands infinitely larger.

If you placed a small particle of matter in absolute space and allowed free fall to take place, the particle would travel in all directions all at once. It would then be converted to energy and become a part of cosmic energy. If you then placed a large fractal of mass particles in absolute space, it would also travel in all directions at once. It would then resemble the movement through space like that of our sun. It would travel in a Fibonacci-type spiraling, ever-outward path.

If one were to imagine the earth traveling around the sun and then imagine traveling back and forth in time, one might find a phenomenon similar to a comet's tail blown by the sun's radiant energy. The phenomenon would materialize and grow in a Fibonacci-type spiral until it fully materialized into the mass of the earth and all of its components. It would then dematerialize but maintain its mass composition into space.

$$FFEME = MC^2 \text{ Hypothesis}$$

Force field energy matrix = mass times the speed of light squared. This is not a nil hypothesis and is open for testing. The free-fall force field energy matrix is the hypothesis to be tested.

$F=E$

Free Fall Equals Energy

Free fall equals energy (the total of all energy). Free fall equals, is the sum total and is the sole source of all energy. $F=E$ is a known law.

Honeycomb Universe

If you try to imagine free fall, you could envision a region encapsulated by a force-field matrix. The region would be made up of many billions of galaxies and be surrounded by an energy matrix. After the galaxies have expanded, the force field should slice through the galaxy regions and become a fiery lavalike flow called an *emollient,* which will produce particles smaller than sound waves but larger than light waves. This is known as *cosmic background radiation.* The actual size of this part of the honeycomb universe can only be described as a *microspeck* on the sharp end of a pin, and even that's too huge a description in an infinite universe. The mechanics would look something like a ring or rubber band stretched to snap, like string theory, and then forming a Milky Way–like formation that condenses and forms an emolument.

Aliens from Outer Space

The fact that light travels 286,000 miles per second, or thirty thousand times faster than any human has traveled, and that the closest solar system with an earthlike planet is five hundred light years away means that travel over that distance would be all but impossible. No human or other world creature would even consider such an impossible adventure.

So, we made a light-emitting space station that travels in all directions. It sends other solar systems light-emitting pulses in code to communicate as much as possible about life on earth. The absolute soonest we could expect a response would be a thousand years from the start of the signals; more likely, it would take tens of thousands or millions of years.

Science Prizes

In the twenty-fourth century achievement prizes were awarded. Most notable was the Rosalind Franklin and Lisa Misner Science Award, which went to the hypothesis of everything and the infinite universe hypothesis. A technology prize, the Nikola Tesla Award, went to Terrane/Tressel Architecture. A peace prize, the Martin Luther King and Mahatma Gandhi, was also awarded each year, along with the Shakespeare Prize for Literature.

TIME TRAVEL

D aniel Morgan's time is a series of events through time and space. That time is a microcosm of the universe. The universe, being infinite, records in real time to the microfraction of a second to infinite smallness. We will take much longer in our own "real time" to present Daniel Morgan's time of 750 years ago.

So, hey, all you time travelers, join us as we race through time between 1776 and 2525! You'll go through our humorous vacations with me, Dooty Grainger, and my colleges, Gaugy, Cary, Drapy, and crazy Early. You'll meet Faith and her family; the medicine-men family of

Running Bear, Little Black Bear, Great Bear, and Great Red Bear; Marnie, her husband, Johann, and her baby; Christine; and Thomas, Larry, and Pete, African American patriots. You'll also meet Michael and David, British expatriates who went AWOL from the British army, Washington's Camp Followers, Dr. Germaine, and the attorney Thomas Summers. Travel the world and the seven seas with Philip Brady. So, hitch a ride with us and let the madcap fun—and a little history—whisk you away. We'll begin our journey with the first part of the American Revolutionary War. Let's get traveling, shall we?

THE COLD WAR

As hostilities, over the years, mounted toward the various acts from the king, including the Stamp Act, the Tea Act, and the Coercive Acts, Governor General Thomas Gage decided he needed to disarm the rebels. This would be carried out with various missions to confiscate powder, cannon, muskets and cannon and musket balls from American stores. His first mission was a powder house on Quarry Hill. The British quietly left Boston in thirteen longboats and rowed toward the Mystic River. When they got ashore, they persuaded the sheriff to give them the keys. They proceeded to Quarry Hill and quickly confiscated 250 half barrels of powder and rowed back to Boston. They were directed to take the powder to Castle William, an island just north of Dorchester. Another detachment rode out to Cambridge and took two cannons that belonged to the province. When the Colonial Whigs learned of this, they were outraged. They were determined not to be outmaneuvered in the future and thus began what was known as the Powder Alarms. General Gage's main adversary was Paul Revere. Revere belonged to the Sons of Liberty club and other groups dedicated to liberty. Both Gage and Revere had spies and were well aware of each other's activity. Gage became even more cautious and secretive. They each had an unsuspected mole close to them. In Gage's case, it was his own wife who was a Whig and had sympathy for both sides. Paul Revere was also in an organization of mechanics (artisans, builders, businessmen, politicians, and engineers), and part of this group was Dr. Warren Church, a spy for General Gage. Revere and the others never suspected him and never learned he was a spy even after the war. Thus, a very short cold war took place.

Portsmouth was the next target of the British. When Revere and the Mechanics learned of this, Revere was immediately sent to warn the town. Revere rode out in midday and warned the town. The result was that a militia of four hundred men was formed, and they proceeded to Fort William and Mary and seized sixteen cannons, sixty muskets, and stores of gunpowder. So, Paul Revere's midday ride may have been as important as his midnight ride. Portsmouth was thought of as a great success for the Colonialists. When the British arrived, they of course came up empty-handed and left Portsmouth swarming with Patriots.

AN EARLY RESULT

E arly was washing his hands, hoping the perceived view of him—psychopath—could be washed away. From out in the hall outside the bathroom, he could hear the request: "Oh, Early, do you have time to come out and talk with us?" *That sounds intriguing*, thought Early. *Maybe washing my hands did the trick?* As he headed out of the bathroom, he felt like this was his lucky day.

As he strolled along the hall, he turned around to see where everyone was; he stumbled backward just as he felt the air in front of him where the poor girls intended blow breezed past, and her wrist slammed into the pillar. As he continued to fall backward, he grabbed onto some hair and yanked the other girl back, straining her neck. His sharp elbow had a direct hit on someone's head. His leg then went out from under him and hit the shin of some poor guy. Finally, he crashed down on someone's back and heard a loud popping sound.

Early strolled out on the promenade, smiling about the fact that he thought he had avoided catastrophe. Not far behind him, after coming out of a first aid station and along next to a yellow revolving lamp, came the five conspirators. First, a guy in a wheelchair, followed by a guy with a broken leg in a cast, a girl with a turban-wrapped bandage on her head, a girl with a tourniquet neck brace, and finally a girl with a broken arm in a cast. A motley crew indeed!

"Hey, Early where have you been?"

"Well, if I missed any excitement, it was due to the fact that I was previously engaged in a small ruse." It seems a merry band of men and women planned a prank, but it seems it backfired.

"You a-hole, have you been practicing your infamous special brand of sociopathy?" exclaimed Cary?"

"Well, I very much wanted to avoid it," claimed Early. "It just wasn't in the cards. No matter how much I washed my hands, I seem to have been touched with Pontius Pilate's knack for retaining guilt despite how many times we wash our hands."

LEXINGTON AND CONCORD

On the morning of April 19, 1775, the Revolutionary War began. There were about seven hundred British soldiers on the Lexington common and about 130 Americans. The British were ordered not to shoot. After sizing up the situation and out of order, the British soldiers, having previously been taunted, decided to charge the Colonialists with bayonets. When they ran, the British became even more incensed by such cowardice after such brave taunts, and they continued to pursue them. Finally, some Americans shot into the British.

Going completely against their orders, a line of British lowered their muskets and shot off a volley. Thus, the war had begun with shots being fired from both sides. It would last seven years and become a global contest. The captain was undeterred and ordered a march to Concord, about two miles further west, to confiscate any muskets, rifles, cannons, and gunpowder. As they approached Concord, both flanking movements and scouts reported hundreds of Colonialists in the hills.

With just three hundred men, the British were now vastly outnumbered. The first thing they did was secure the Concord River and the North and South Bridges while they were still out of range of the Americans. When the British destroyed two cannons, they set the carriages on fire, which accidentally started some houses on fire. The colonel quickly started a bucket brigade and put the fires out.

The Colonialists noticed the smoke and started to act. The British saw hundreds of Colonialists approaching the North Bridge and fled to a ridge just beyond the bridge. They formed a tight formation so they could have revolving lines to rapidly reload for continuous fire. Shots rang out as the British became nervous, and they also found themselves too tightly packed to rotate to the front line. The Colonialists started volleys and totally decimated the British.

As they retreated, the colonel came back to find his four companies of light infantry, which had been sent beyond the North Bridge to the Barrett house, which was supposed to store munitions. When the companies arrived at the bridge, the Colonists separated and allowed them to pass. They still didn't want to attack unless provoked by the British.

The colonel ordered a march back to Lexington. All this effort resulted in just two cannons being disabled since the Colonists had already secured most of their powder and munitions.

The weapons of those days consisted of muskets with bayonets and long rifles that were more accurate. Muskets only took about fifteen seconds to reload, but rifles took a full minute. Colonialists were generally better shots as frontier life and hunting required such skill to survive. Although the Colonialists would eventually have rifle divisions, most of the New Englanders had various types of muskets, mostly without bayonets. The British used muskets with bayonets.

The march back to Lexington found the British often nearly surrounded. As Colonial militias started to arrive, the British ran into at least eight ambushes along the road. They were nearly wiped out and ready to surrender. As they reentered Lexington, they found that the reserves had arrived with nearly 1,700 troops.

For the Colonialists, Lexington awaited a new general. General Heath was a well-known tactician of warfare, especially in the

Americas. He would organize a fast-moving skirmish that devastated the slow-moving British lines. The British could now begin their march back to Charleston and Boston with a decent-sized force. This was, however, in the face of the swelling Colonial force, which was now in the thousands.

The march back to Boston was a repeat of the one from Concord to Lexington. As the British marched, the Colonialists used a continual circling movement called a ring of fire, shooting from behind trees, hedges, and fences. The British countered that by deploying flanking movements that caught Americans by surprise and either used their bayonets or shot musket balls into their faces.

The British searched houses that were suspected of shooting at them and bayoneted or shot any inhabitants. Since the rear flank was taking most of the casualties, the British started to rotate the formations to the rear. As the British came closer to Charleston, they found that the Colonists had completely disabled the bridge they needed to cross. Instead, they took a fork to the south that was little used or known about.

At last, they arrived in Charleston and began ferrying troops over to Boston. The British suffered nearly one hundred casualties with probably forty to forty-five dead. It can probably be assumed the Colonialists had a similar if not greater loss. The deployment by Colonialists of fast moving skirmishing tactics and the British answer of light infantry would play out throughout the war.

BREEDS HILL

Colonial forces quickly surrounded Boston, but they were hardly able to mount a siege since they were without cannons. The British held onto Charleston and Boston. The Colonialists completely surrounded the city and began building defenses and redoubts north of Charleston at Breeds Hill, which was just below Bunker Hill. The redoubts and ditches faced east, south, and west. A reinforced picket fence went from a breastwork eastward down to the beach on Mystic River. The breastwork went north and south and looked down on the beach.

The Colonialists were in place, digging their defenses and getting shelled by British ships awaiting the British Army. As the shelling continued, many of the Colonial militia began to depart. There was some leaving because they were afraid and others who simply wanted to go home. Replacements were sought from other counties, but the Colonialists numbers were reduced. The Colonialists would eventually outnumber the British with about 3,500 compared to 2,500 of the enemy.

The big day came on June 17, 1775. The British ferried their troops who were under the command of General Howe. Howe took a good look at the battlefield and decided on his strategy. He decided to attack along the beach in thin columns and destroy the picket fence and form a flanking movement to cut off the Colonialists from the rear. One of the many problems with that was that he could not see the breastworks looking down on the beach because they were hidden behind Breeds Hill. He would then attack with his main column directly at the redoubts of Breeds Hill. The orders were given out, and so began the epic battle, which was later called Bunker Hill.

Two companies of light infantry of the Twenty-Third, the Fusiliers—perhaps the most famous of British troops—began the attack. The column was thin, and there was too little space front to back. They were followed by many more troops. Although this company was famous, these particular troops had little experience and had only recently been trained. As they approached the Colonialists, they began firing against their orders, and as usual, it was to no avail.

The Colonialists let out a crushing volley that felled most of the troops on early approach. This was followed by raking volleys sent down from the breastworks. It was almost hard to miss as long as you lowered your gun properly. The rifles along the picket fence, taking at least a full minute to reload, allowed the British to regroup and continue the attack. This also allowed the Colonialists to recognize the officers ordering the men. The next volley made a good target for the officers, killing eight of the ten there. The British were returning fire at this point, but the rounds were soaring overhead, probably between one and five feet. This only allowed the Colonialist's time to reload the breastworks and continue to pound the British from flank. Howe immediately noticed his mistake, but there was no plan B.

After about half an hour—and with two aides shot standing right next to him—Howe finally got off orders for a new battle plan. He would attack Breeds from the left and the right. His main force would come up from the left, and the two remaining companies would attack from the right.

As the British closed in on the redoubts, they found themselves less exposed to fire, and the Americans started to waste shots and balls.

As the British consolidated right below their redoubt, the Americans were running out of ammunition and then retreating to the rear for passage over Bunker Hill, signaling the end of the battle.

The British filled the redoubts and last made good use of their bayonets running through any remaining unlucky soldiers. The British won the field, but at what cost? The British had more than nine hundred casualties with about 226 dead. The officers suffered disproportionately with nineteen killed and seventy wounded. The Americans suffered casualties probably less than half that of the British. So, Bunker Hill became a sore spot for the British and a rallying cry for the Americans.

THE BLIND SAMURAI

He had his sword in both hands pointed upward while sitting in his seat. The sword had a sonic blade that was an ionic beam that looked just like real steel. As they disembarked the tube, first came a man in a wheelchair followed by a man with a broken leg followed by a woman with a turban-like bandage on her followed by a woman with a neck brace followed by a woman with a broken arm in a cast. They were followed by a man with a shifty nature; he was known as Early.

He was followed by the Blind Samurai. The five handicapped people kept a wistful eye on Early, but he was assessing the Blind Samurai.

The Blind Samurai moved up quickly on Early and cut off his head. The five handicapped people seemed relieved. Soon, the Blind Samurai narrowed in on his next target, the five handicapped people, and proceeded to hack them to pieces.

In the meantime, four of the five documentary historians were watching *It's a Gift,* an old film with W. C. Fields. Fields was saying to quickly open the doors because the blind house detective from the hotel across the street was coming over. The detective was easily evading the cars in the street. The doors were open, and Fields settled back to relax.

Just then, his assistant came in and closed the doors.

The blind detective smashed the windows of both doors. When he came in, he shouted, "Who closed those doors again?"

Fields looked at his assistant and softly proclaimed, "I hate you!"

The blind detective settled into his usual chair, but the assistant had put a display table full of light bulbs in front of the detective's chair. The detective started swinging his cane, just missing the light bulbs as he swung back and forth.

"Be careful, Mr. Muckle. Be careful, Mr. Muckle, dear."

Just then, the blind detective leveled his cane and shattered all the light bulbs on display. Once again, Fields softly proclaimed to his assistant, "I hate you!"

So, the historic documenters had a table with rubber light bulbs on display. The Blind Samurai quietly stepped into the historians' workplace and proceeded to hack them to pieces. He then stomped up to the table with the rubber light bulbs and hacked them to pieces along with the table. His bloodlust not satisfied, he slithered along the mall and found a group of insurance adjusters. He left them in small pieces. He finally felt satisfied and slipped quietly into his suite, which was a metal shop.

After having his head cut off, Early sauntered up the hall and into the mall. He rounded the corner and headed into the documentary production room. "It's a good thing the Blind Samurai has a beam on that sword instead of a real steel blade."

Car-y said, "Oh, I'm sure you would have loved the mayhem, yourself excluded, of course. A true psychopath."

"Speak for yourself, Car-y. I'm sure you would have delighted in a little mayhem, especially if any verbal abuse was involved."

Drapey had his best outfit depicting Paul Revere. "You know, Paul had ridden for several days on his minutemen alarm without washing and stunk to high heaven. His fellow Patriots had arranged a meeting now that Samuel Adams was back. They invited Paul into the tavern, but they soon found the odor unbearable. As they commenced outside and seated Paul on the outside of the table, they were able to just bear up to the stink!

As Drapey emerged from the documentary suite, he found a familiar group: a man in a wheelchair, a man with a broken leg, a woman with a tourniquet on her neck, a woman with a turbanlike bandage on her head, and a woman with her arm in a cast. For some reason, they all wore gas masks.

BOSTON LIBERATED

On July 3, 1775, George Washington took command of the army. He soon found out that the men generally had a great fighting spirit, but they had inexperienced, poor officers to lead them. Since most militias were voluntary from the same areas, they usually just voted for their most popular peers to lead them. This was not exactly the recipe for the discipline needed for an army. The militia was gradually replaced with new continental companies from all thirteen states. Although the quality and training of these troops was in doubt, the new army was beginning to form.

The British were being starved off the peninsula, but on October 6, 1775, the *Cerberus* sailed into Boston Harbor with plenty of food and supplies. They also had an order that relieved General Gage of duty and made General Howe the new commander of the army. The British started to make preparations to leave Boston, but it took some time.

On March 5, 1776, Washington was seen on Dorchester Heights with heavy cannon sure to follow. The British were to attack the hill, but a huge gale blew up and prevented crossing to Dorchester Heights. Finally, on March 20, there were loud explosions. The British were blowing up their own fort at Castle Williams and also their barracks in Charleston.

Within three weeks, the British were gone. More than ninety men of war and transports were taking the British to Halifax, Nova Scotia.

Invasion of Canada

The Continental Congress began to set their sights on Canada. They sent messages to the French Canadians to join their cause opposing the British. It would seem they might be receptive, but the Congress had misread them. First of all, they were being treated well by the British, and secondly, they knew the Colonialists did not like Catholics and were reluctant to participate with their adversaries. Thus, the Americans would have to invade Canada on their own and hope the Canadians would go along. So, sometime after this and May 1775, the Congress authorized the invasion of Canada.

The Congress authorized the army in June 1775 and placed George Washington as its head. They put Philip Schuyler in charge in northern New York. Ethan Allen and the Green Mountain Boys along with Benedict Arnold and the Connecticut Militia had already secured Ticonderoga. Schuyler was directed to invade Canada. Washington received a letter from Arnold recommending another mission to Canada through the Maine wilderness.

Washington approved a plan where Arnold and Major Daniel Morgan—along with 1,100 soldiers—would use the rivers in Maine for a second campaign to Canada. Ethan Allen became ill on the campaign to Saint-Jean and was replaced by General Richard Montgomery.

Montgomery laid siege to Saint-Jean, and it surrendered on November 2. In the meantime, Allen set about to raid Montreal. He was repulsed by General Guy Carleton and was himself captured. After capturing Saint-Jean, Montgomery proceeded to Montreal and captured the city along with a small flotilla. He then left a small garrison and followed Carleton to Quebec City.

On September 12, Arnold and his men left Cambridge, Massachusetts, by sea and proceeded north to the Penobscot River. They would proceed north as far as the river would take them and then march onto the Chaudière River, flowing toward Saint Lawrence River. Before they reached the Chaudière, they had lost more than half their men to disease or desertion. They finally arrived west of Quebec City on the Saint Lawrence on November 8. They crossed the river and set up a blockade. Carleton managed to evade them and started to set up a defense of the city. Montgomery arrived outside of the city on December 3. Combining the two forces left them with only 1,100 men.

On December 31, they attacked the city. Carleton was aware they would attempt a foul-weather assault and prepared the garrison of some 1,800 men for the assault. After just a short while, Montgomery was dead—and Arnold was badly wounded.

Morgan continued on and made his way inside the city, but he was promptly surrounded and had to surrender along with 450 men. Arnold managed to take the rest of the force about a mile west of the city and remained there under miserable conditions until he was relieved in April 1776. Morgan and most of his men were eventually let go and repatriated. So, the invasion of Canada was over, and it was a disaster for the colonies. The Colonialists retreated back to Ticonderoga.

Dooty

All of the world's top mathematicians were invited to the Biennial Mathematical Contest. This year's title is the "Yentls of Yalta" being held, of course, in Yalta, Ukraine, on the Baltic Sea. That year, the contest was to solve the Hodge conjecture. The winner of the contest, Jersy Osiak of Poland, made no mistakes. In second place, Nikita Zhukov of Russia made one mistake, and in third place, Dooty Grainger made two mistakes.

The Yentls of Yalta became a regular Babs festival. Dooty was Babs as Yentl. Gaughy was Babs as Fanny Brice. Cary was just plain ole Babs, Barbara Streisand, Drapey was Babs's weird uncle in *On a Clear Day You Can See Forever*, a part played by Jack Nicholson, and Early was playing Barbara's lover in *The Way We Were*, a part played by Robert Redford.

Not to be outdone by the mathematical competition, the Great Mathematician decided to throw a big party in Napoleon's time period, featuring Napoleon's assassination. A Barbara Streisand (lookalike) was playing Josephine, who died in 1814, seven years before Napoleon died. She also plays Yentl, a woman dressed as a man since women weren't allowed to study the Jewish Old Testament. Danika Mc Keller (a lookalike) was playing Marie Antoinette. Jennifer Lawrence (a lookalike) was playing one of Benjamin Franklin's mistresses. Lindsey Lohan (lookalike) was playing the duchess of Devonshire. Leonardo De Caprio (a lookalike) was playing Napoleon. Finally, Brad Pitt (a lookalike) was playing King George III.

At the dance, Marie Antoinette said, "Looking around, I hardly see anyone making 100,000 French francs." She further iterated, "Let them eat cake."

The duchess of Devonshire (known for excessive gambling, drinking, smoking, drugs like snorting cocaine, numerous men, and general debauchery) said, "And let them eat wholeheartedly, drink excessively, gamble wholeheartedly, make love whenever, and generally have a good time.

Not to be caught off guard, Ben's mistress said, "Let the games begin, dah-linck." Of course, the young emperor chimed in with his charming wit and said, "Dear ones and old warriors, let us take them in battle; form up square regiments, firing from all sides, and slay the infidels after which we can eat, drink, and be merry—not to mention then tomorrow we shall die."

Lastly, old King George (occasionally remembering his own name) said, "I have a whole library full of books telling us to be pious, but, by golly, let your wickedness save your ass." Of course, King George was just placating the duchess, much to his wife's chagrin. He did not, in fact, gamble, drink, smoke, do drugs, or womanize. After all, his wife bore him fifteen children with thirteen surviving. King George and Lady Charlotte decided to play bridge with Napoleon and Josephine.

"By George, I believe that is a trump," declared Napoleon.

In the meantime, the lovely duchess was killing it and winning all the hands she played in the blackjack poker game. She was, in fact, playing by number counting, illegal today but not even known back then.

Napoleon died of arsenic poisoning while in exile on St. Helena Island. That year's murder mystery was guessing who killed Napoleon (among his closest staff) and why he was killed. To cut her losses short, the mistress persuaded everyone to bet on who was guilty of the arsenic poisoning. To further cut her losses, she chose what she thought was a sure bet: the Comte de Montholo.

Napoleon, particularly perplexed, perhaps because he was already dead, chose Sir Hudson Lowe. Napoleon detested his "jailer," the man who became governor of St. Helena in April 1816. He was supposed to make Napoleon's life easier, but he made his life miserable. He couldn't even get his much-needed exercise horseback riding without Lowe spying on him.

Lowe was a former commander of the Corsican Rangers, avowed enemies of the Bonaparte family. So, the roots of hatred ran deep. King George, always ready to cast aspersions on the French, chose Baron Gourgaud. Queen Charlotte also chose a Frenchie and his slut wife:

General Count Henri-Gatien Bertrand and Countess Francois-Elisabeth (Fanny) Bertrand. "They should have fried her fanny," said the ever-charming Charlotte.

Marie Antoinette, also long since dead, decided to go for the usual suspect. "The butler did it," declared Marie. "Just more of those lower-class troglodytes."

Louis Marchand, the emperor's loyal valet of ten years, certainly had the means and opportunity.

Finally, Josephine, long since dead, liking the slut debauchery angle as well, chose the duchess of Devonshire—even though she was, in fact, never on St. Helena. What the hell? The empress was already dead anyway—so give her a hand for her creativity at least!

There are several suspects for the arsenic poisoning and subsequent murder of Napoleon Bonaparte. To be a suspect, the person had to have been with Napoleon for the first five years, especially in the past eighteen months when the full administration of the arsenic poisoning took place. They also needed a good motive.

The first of these was General Count Henri-Gatien Bertrand and his wife, Countess Fanny Bertrand. They were there during the entire time of Napoleon's exile, and they were always in contact with him.

General Count Henri-Gatien Bertrand was Napoleon's grand marshal of the palace every day.

Countess Bertrand hated the island and said, "The devil shit this place as he flew from one continent to the other." Loyal to her husband, she stayed by his side until Napoleon's death on May 5, 1821. She was at the ex-emperor's bedside when he died.

These eyewitnesses were all companions of Napoleon and C. Baron Gourgaud, one of Napoleon's long-serving officers, who had followed him into exile. The current government of France would have had an interest in seeing to it that Napoleon would not regain his power. That would have been enough motivation to murder Napoleon, and they could have bribed Gourgaud to do the dirty deed.

Other suspects included Dr. Barry O'Meara, an English doctor of Irish descent, who was appointed by the English to act as the emperor's physician, and Dr. Francesco Antommarchi, an Italian physician sent by Napoleon's family in Rome to replace O'Meara when he was sent home to England. Britain would have also had a good motive to kill Napoleon. These two doctors were not on the scene the entire time that Napoleon was in exile and were therefore not good suspects.

Walter Henry and John Stokoe were English doctors who attended to Napoleon for short periods. They were not with Napoleon the entire time of his exile and therefore were not suspects.

Louis Marchand, the emperor's loyal valet of ten years, had direct and intimate contact with Napoleon and could have been bribed by the French. These eight people had regular access to Napoleon and observed him on a daily basis, and they all kept independent diaries of their lives on St. Helena.

The Comte de Montholon, on the other hand, had no reason to admire or wish to serve the emperor on St. Helena, yet he volunteered his services to do so. Napoleon was only forty-six years old at the time, and he was in good health. He could have lived at least another twenty years, which meant that Montholon might have had to spend a good part of his life serving him.

Unless he was an agent of the Bourbons and knew in advance that he would need to spend only a few years on the island because of his assignment to poison Napoleon, there would be no logical reason for him to do this.

Comte de Montholon was raised bearing the name Montholon-Simonville. However, when he left to go to St. Helena, he very cleverly dropped the Simonville part of his name and went simply as Comte de Montholon. Montholon was known as a playboy, was always in debt, and enjoyed the fast life. Why would a man with that background want to spend at least twenty years of his life serving Napoleon on St. Helena unless he had specific orders to prevent Napoleon from returning to France by poisoning him?

Consider that the Comte de Montholon was the sommelier and had exclusive access to Napoleon's wine. It was through the wine that Napoleon was poisoned. Arsenic powder is neutral—it has no taste—and it could have been put into his wine whenever Montholon wanted to.

In fact, Baron Gourgaud, in his memoirs, recorded that he warned Napoleon that he might be poisoned through the wine. However, Napoleon did not take this warning seriously. Consider also that Montholon was a major beneficiary of Napoleon's will and was appointed one of the three executors. Montholon was alone with Napoleon when he prepared his last will and added codicils. Montholon was actually left more than 2,200,000 francs, a huge amount of money in those days, and yet he was bankrupt and had to flee to Belgium to escape his creditors in 1829.

Montholon was upset with Napoleon because he had ordered Montholon's discharge from his post as the French envoy to Wurzburg after he married the twice-divorced Albine Roger against Napoleon's wishes.

During his stay at the defense establishment in 1814, while Napoleon was in exile in Elba, Montholon had appropriated to himself some military funds amounting to six thousand francs. However, he was never punished for this crime, thanks to the intervention of the Comte d'Artois, who later became Charles X, the king of France.

Louis XVIII appointed the Comte de Montholon, a French general during Napoleon's exile on Elba. All historians, even those who don't agree that Napoleon was poisoned, agree that Montholon was a very scheming and unscrupulous man who lied on a regular basis. After everyone returned from St. Helena, the Count Montholon visited Italy on several occasions. He frequently visited a direct descendant of Louis XIV who would later become king of France. His name on being crowned King was Charles X.

Well, it is not always the obvious suspect who commits the dirty deed! In some cases, it is the person or persons you least expect. Count Bertrand and his wife were with Napoleon the entire time he was in exile. They were in direct contact with Napoleon on an almost hourly basis. It was said the countess was Napoleon's lover, and she did, in fact, give him his baths. They could easily have been bribed by the French. However, it was not they who poisoned Napoleon, and the countess was not his lover—but she did give Napoleon his baths.

No, in fact, in this case, it *was* the most obvious suspect who poisoned Napoleon. It was, in fact, the descendants of Louis XVI who bribed the count by paying off his debts. The motive was revenge!

In the morning, Dooty woke up and prepared to go home. When she went down to the lobby, she found out that the mathematical committee had made a mistake. Dooty and the Russian had made no mistakes, after all, and they shared the first prize with Jersy Osiak.

Dooty took the tube to the Alps high plains and then took the space elevator to dock. She then rode the space tube to the Albuquerque dock and descended to Albuquerque and onto the tube to LA. It was a fun and rewarding trip!

New York, New York

The Halifax regimen, with 130 ships and 9,300 men, arrived at Staten Island on July 2, 1776. Ten days later, Admiral Howe, the commander's brother, and 150 ships sailed into Staten Island. In all, the British would field thirty-two thousand soldiers for its New York conquest.

Washington anticipated the British invasion of New York and marched most of his troops from Boston to New York. He knew the odds were overwhelmingly against him, but the Congress had ordered the defense of New York.

By the time the British were in place, Washington could only muster about twenty thousand troops. To defend the city, Washington sent three of his five divisions to Long Island around Brooklyn. This included General Green, General Putnam, and Major General Sullivan. The British had been building small sloops to carry their troops from Staten Island to Long Island, and it was no surprise from where they were coming.

Finally, on August 22, the British sent a force of fifteen thousand troops onto Long Island. Under the command of Cornwallis, they quickly took Flatbush to face off the defenses in front of Brooklyn. This was followed by five thousand Hessian troops landing on Long

Island two days later. The stage was set for the British to initiate the battle.

Howe decided to use a flank attack on their left side to envelop the Colonialists. He sent General Clinton on the evening of the twenty-sixth on the flanking maneuver. So, on the twenty-seventh, the battle quickly commenced. A diversionary attack was started on the right and moved to the middle. As Clinton's troops engaged, Sullivan panicked by the surprise rear attack. He would have known earlier, but Putnam had failed to communicate.

The efforts of Brigadier General Alexander, nicknamed Lord Stirling, saved the day. He found the only escape across a swamp, and he positioned a detachment that he commanded to temporarily attack Clinton while the rest of the men retreated. It was successful, but Lord Stirling and his men had to surrender.

Washington was witnessing this from General Putnam's headquarters, and by midday, he realized that Howe would lay siege to Brooklyn. He decided to evacuate his troops, but with so many Tory spies, he held off telling his senior officers until late in the evening. The men were told they were being relieved from Manhattan. A force of two thousand would cover the withdrawal across the East River using fishing boats.

When the British finally learned that the Americans had abandoned their positions, it was too late. They arrived in time to see the last boat, carrying General Washington, headed for Manhattan at around seven o'clock the next morning on August 28.

On September 15, the British decided to make their assault on Manhattan. They landed at Kips Bay and proceeded to rout the fleeing Americans. George Washington got off his horse, threw his hat, and cursed his troops. Fortunately, his aides seized his horse and led him to safety as musket balls whizzed past them. Washington then ordered his troops to prepare entrenchments at Harlem Heights.

Lieutenant Colonel Thomas Knowlton and a battalion of about 150 rangers began to reconnoiter Hallows Way just below Harlem

Heights. Washington ordered him to go with Colonel Weedon to go around the British left flank. At the same time, the remainder of Weedon's troops were to attack the British with musket fire from the front. The frontal attack worked well, but the left flank started firing too soon—much to Washington's annoyance. Either George Putnam or Brigadier General George Clinton volunteered to accompany that left flank. That flank was not supposed to fire until after they reached the British rear. The British had to retreat back to high ground on Hollow Way. Knowlton and Weedon fell mortally wounded. The British sent General Alexander Leslie to reinforce the British. The British still had to retreat with Americans in pursuit.

At that point, nearly five thousand troops were engaged on each side. The British lost two hundred wounded and seventy killed. The Americans had thirty killed and ninety wounded. General Howe planned his next move and decided not to advance on the American entrenchments. Two weeks went by, and a great fire was started in New York. Howe was furious and ended up having Nathan Hale hanged without a trial for spying. He stated famously, "I regret that I have but one life to give for my country."

White Plains, New York

When General Howe finally decided to use his naval advantage, Washington decided it was time to give up Manhattan. The withdrawal took place ahead of Howe's naval procurement and headed for White Plains. Howe's move came a month later. On October 12, he left half his army in Manhattan and took the other ten thousand up the East River on the Bronx shore known as Throggs Neck. He did not want to divide his army too far and ended up landing too close to the Americans.

Cornwallis was thus held upon the peninsula defended well by Colonel Edward Hand and the Pennsylvania Rifle Regiment; 1,800 Americans ended up holding the British on the narrow neck on and about a square mile of area. As Howe moved toward White Plains, he began small skirmishes with the Americans, avoiding a direct assault.

After the small battle, Washington moved his troops north of White Plains to a new position between the Bronx River and St. Mary Lake. For three days, the two armies faced off, and then Washington withdrew again by night to Castle Heights.

The British went as far as White Plains and finally decided to withdraw entirely back to Manhattan and start a siege on Fort Washington where two thousand American troops remained. The final tally was 250 of American losses with fifty killed; the British had a similar outcome.

FORT WASHINGTON

General Howe assembled eight thousand troops to assault Fort Washington under General Rall. The main thrust would be from the north with three thousand men under General Knyphausen. From the east, another three thousand troops in two columns were led by Mathew and Cornwallis. Lord Percy, advancing from the south with another two thousand troops, would complete the attack force.

Fort Washington overlooked a bluff 230 feet above the Hudson. It was a simple earthwork pentagon. Colonel Robert Magaw was the garrison commander. Washington doubted it could hold against a British attack, but Green, Putnam, and Magaw all thought they could hold it. On November 16, 1776, at ten in the morning, the German forces from the north began the attack, followed by Cornwallis and Mathew from the east, and finally all four divisions were on the attack.

When Magaw realized his position was hopeless, he tried to discuss surrender terms with Rall. Washington sent a message to hold out until nightfall, but it was already too late. Magaw had already surrendered. The Americans lost fifty-three killed, ninety-six wounded, and 2,722 captured. The British lost seventy-seven killed, 374 wounded, and seven missing. They also captured forty-three artillery pieces. Once again, Washington had been outmanned and out-generaled. He had listened to his subordinates—Greene, Putnam, and Maga—and as a result, he lost nearly half his army. Although it was upon his subordinate's advice, he alone was responsible and would have to bear the consequences.

FORT LEE

T he whole purpose of the Continental Congress authorizing the building Forts Washington and Lee was to prevent the British Navy from moving up the Hudson. Although Washington was ordered to defend the forts, that became superfluous after Fort Washington fell. The British had no problem sailing up the Hudson even with the forts fully employed.

Washington ordered Greene to retreat from Fort Lee. The army north of New York stayed where they were, but the New Jersey army retreated south all the way to the Delaware River. They crossed the river and confiscated all the riverboats. The British quickly occupied most of New Jersey. The fighting was seemingly over for the year, and the armies went into winter quarters.

FAITH

"Faith, dear, why are you always playing with those tops?"
"Well, Lauren, they are my experimental representations of our rotating and orbiting earth and the earth's gravitational pull to the sun. There is one orbiting movement, and there are two rotating movements. Each of these movements changes in regular cycles, probably short, medium, and long. The long one, I'll call eccentricity in that earth goes from a nearly perfect round orbit to an elliptical orbit. Another is a wobbling rotation, just like when a top slows down. A third is an incline change of the earth's orbit, exposing the Southern Hemisphere to more territorial sunshine. All three of these would affect the temperature on earth, and it will be much colder than it is today."

"Faith, dear, with all that wobbling, why aren't we being thrown off the earth?" "Well, Lauren, dear, the earth has an air atmosphere, and the gravitational pull of the sun prevents us from being pulled into space."

"Well, Faith, dear, while that may make sense to you, I think God's plan is much different. When Father God takes the sun lamp across the sky, it provides us with light and warmth. How could the earth be attracted to a lantern?"

"Lauren, what happens to the sun when night falls?"

"Well, Faith, Father God takes the sun lantern underground and brings it out of the tunnel the very next day. During the night, the archangels hold lanterns far up in the sky and provide us with beautiful starlight."

"Well, Lauren, if God is so busy with those lanterns, how does he control the rest of the universe?"

"Silly girl, God is everywhere and everything at the same time. He is even the archangels and the universe. Piece of cake."

"Well, Lauren, I guess that explains it."

Mrs. Stevens said, "Faith, dear, it's time to empty the nighttime bedpans." "Yes, Mrs. Stevens, I remember." Faith empties the bedpans, washes her hands, and returns to the kitchen. "Hiya, Gramma Opra. Where is everybody?"

"Well, your mother is out at the outhouse, and your father is out in the field of course." Just then, Tom ran into the kitchen and said, "Well, the older brother has gone and done it now! He done wop Joseph with his evil whip at least a hundred times. He said Joseph and his crew is not harvesting fast enough. My heavens, he done him good! Sorry, Faith, dear. Here he comes now."

"Oh, Papa, what has he done to you?"

"Faith, dear daughter, it was just a misunderstanding. Your papa will be all right." Faith's momma came in and fainted.

"Papa, I'll sting your wounds with some alcohol. Then I'll put some molasses and honey on your back as a kind of a salve on your back—unless Gramma Opra has some of her special blend."

"Faith, dear, I gave my portion to Colonel Morgan, but we can retrieve it tomorrow. Meanwhile, I've got to attend to your poor momma. She's had quite a shock, poor dear." "Come on, Papa. Let's tend to your wounds."

GAUGY

augy was recruited by the foreign service and went to Washington to be trained as a special agent. She was trained to intercept other foreign agents, and she was assigned to Vienna. Vienna was known as the spy capital of the world and had numerous coffeehouses where the spies could congregate.

Gaughy made it to an outside table at one of the bistros. She ordered a doppio macchiato and a pastry and waited for some prospects. The spies were all aware why everyone was there; it was a tit-for-tat arrangement. She soon had good company.

"Hello, dear. May we sit down?" asked Natasha.

"Be my guests," said Gaughy.

Boris and Natasha sat down and ordered drinks and food.

Gaughy and her friends spoke about the ongoing mix-and-match robotic military chess game. They invited him up to their room.

"Don't forget the password, Dah-link."

Gaughy knocked on the door.

"Flying squirrel?"

Gaughy thought about it and replied, "Rocky?"

"Echelenta, dah-link!" Natasha opened the door.

"Who is it, Mishka?" asked Boris.

"It's that beautiful blonde American, dah-link," replied Natasha.

"Oh great!" exclaimed Boris. "Come in, dear, and have some vodka and caviar." After a toast, he added, "Are you after some robot codes, my dear Gaughy?"

"Oh, yes. That would be great. With the robotic party, it would be nice to have the most up-to-date codes on the most up-to-date equipment just to stay even. That's only fair, isn't it?" "Of course, dah-link, everyone likes to stay up to date," replied Natasha.

They had more to eat and drink, and Gaughy decided to retire for the evening. "We'll be going to the casino in the morning, dah-link. Would you like to join us?" "Sounds like fun!"

"OK, we'll meet you at nine thirty in the lobby."

"Sounds like a winner!"

The next morning, Gaughy got up early, grabbed some coffee, and went to the casino. She was taken to the surveillance room to look at old tapes of Boris and Natasha gambling. The card expert told her that Natasha and Boris were experts at card counting, but they couldn't nab them since they always played the last five hands squarely.

"They may win or lose on the last of the deck, but it's confounding since we don't know what they're up to."

Gaughy went back to the hotel and ate ham and eggs with hash browns and sourdough toast with another doppio macchiato. She went to her room, dressed in her sexiest outfit, and went down to the lobby. She met Boris and Natasha and they took a limo to the casino.

Natasha started gambling at the blackjack table, and Boris followed suit on another table. For a while, Gaughy watched Natasha winning on certain hands and folding on uncertain ones. Gaughy started playing at another table and did pretty well to stay even. Boris and Natasha were winning every hand they played. She could see what the surveillance expert was talking about. She noticed they both played the last hands straight, winning some and losing some as if they didn't care. That threw the card expert off since they sometimes had big losses.

Gaughy proceeded to the casino lounge and ordered a dry martini, chicken wings, fries, and quesadillas with pepperoncini and salsa. When she looked at the cameras again, she realized that the feed must go somewhere.

The bartender told her it went to all the other casinos all over the world.

That evening, she went to Boris and Natasha's room and knocked. Natasha answered, "Moose."

Gaughy replied, "Bullwinkle."

"Dah-link, come in please."

"I wondered if I could talk to you about how to win at blackjack."

"Sure," said Boris. "We use a numbering system that is guaranteed to win; however, so we don't get caught, we play the last five hands straight up. Depending on how much risk we want to take on, we can end up losing or winning on the night. Do you think the surveillance people use codes to detect cheating?"

"Of course, dah-link, they can use Fibonacci, fractals, or quadratics and easily spot cheaters. That's why we play the last five straight."

Back in her room, Gaughy contacted her superiors and asked if there was a casino near Colorado Springs.

"Well, yeah," said the chief. "There is an Indian casino near the military base." She asked if they could make a list of all the military personnel who frequented the place.

The next morning, she got her answer. On the list, there was a lieutenant who worked in the robotic positioning unit.

"You may want to interview the soldier and see what he knows."

Gaughy went to breakfast and had an espresso and some eggs and pancakes. She met Boris and Natasha in the lobby, and they headed for the casino for another day of gambling. "So, you work for the American embassy, dah-link?"

"Yes, of course!"

"We work for the Moldvannia embassy as well."

"So, we both work for our governments."

"Yes, Vienna is known as the spy capital of the world—hint, hint—but we're just government employees serving our respective nations,"

Boris said, "Our great leader, Heir Titlear, holds the balance of robotic military opposing forces.

"So, if one side gained a significant edge in their forces, they could control the opposing forces?"

"Yes, dah-link. In theory anyway, but no country would seek to exploit that advantage because the opposing forces could rearrange their forces and wipe out anyone who attempted such folly. That would effectively put them out of the game. They would be ostracized by all other nations. It's a losing battle that no one wants."

In Colorado Springs, the lieutenant was interrogated. He was writing down all the hands Boris and Natasha were playing and was giving the strategy to the head of Centcom, General "Screaming Meamie" Wieskoff. He thought she was just an avid card player.

When this news was conveyed back to Gaughy, it was game time! However, her Moldvannia cohorts said there could never be an advantage because the forces would just switch sides. She finally figured out that once the battle was engaged, one unit against another, the first two would have a loser. If the timing was right, there could be no shifting of forces until the next units engaged. So, if the second two had the same winners and losers on the respective sides, it would catapult and end up with just one set of winners and one set of losers. Gaugy thought, *Huh? Titlear, Screaming Meamie, and Boris and Natasha would control the world.*

Gaughy quickly flew back to Washington to be debriefed by her superiors. Centcom would have to retrieve the codes and thwart a battle. The actual plan was even easier than Gaughy envisioned. The first robotic military of Titlear would be larger than Centcom. It would take it out easily with the codes supplied by Natasha and Boris. The other robotic militaries would take each other out, and Titlear larger would finish off the last one. Titlear would control the world.

Screaming Meamie was relieved of her command and placed in a high-security prison. Boris and NaTasha were intercepted in Vienna, arrested, and sent to the Hague. The general and the two spies confessed, and Heir Titlear was removed from power. Within weeks, a new democratic government was voted in in Molvannia.

Titlear, Boris and Natasha, and Screaming Meamie were tried and convicted of espionage, conspiracy, and attempted control of world government.

"Dah-link, we're being sent to a country club prison. We'll have all the food and drink we could possibly want, tennis courts, swimming pools, bowling alleys, and basketball courts. Thank you so much, dah-link. You're always looking out for me."

"Your welcome, Mishka. Nothing's good for you."

Natasha and Boris looked over at Titlear and Screaming Meamie and said, "We'll see you on the mixed doubles courts, dah-links!"

Gaugy went back to Washington to report. She tubed to her day job in LA with the Daniel Morgan Historical Project.

TRENTON AND PRINCETON

So far, 1776 had been a very good year for the British. They occupied New York City and most of New Jersey, and planning for 1777 was now in order. The British went into winter quarters, which included a Hessian division of some three thousand men stationed in and around Trenton and Bordentown. Washington had about 2,400 men who were joined by another two thousand Pennsylvania militia on temporary duty.

In a daring move, Washington planned an attack on Christmas Day. They were targeting Trenton and Bordentown and then on to New Brunswick where they could find food, clothing, and ammunition. In terrible weather, which included wind, rain, sleet, and snow flurries, Washington got his 2,400 men across the river. Ice cakes bobbed against the fifty-foot slopes that were used to cross. They also had eighteen field pieces.

The Pennsylvania units, under Ewing and Cadwallader, failed to accomplish their part of the mission and remained on the west bank. Ewing gave up entirely, and Cadwallader made only a timid attempt. Washington would have to go it alone. Washington's troops were split into two columns. Greene's division took the more easterly route along Pennington Road. Sullivan came along River Road.

In Trenton, Johann Rall, a Hessian colonel, made no attempt to fortify his position because he had no respect for the Americans. His only measure to secure his position was to post pickets. The pickets did their job, but it was too late. As they retreated toward the city to sound the alarm, the Patriots surged in from both roads. The muskets were too wet to fire, and the cannons were used ahead of bayonets. Rall and Lossberg's regiments surrendered to Greene's men in a field east of Trenton.

The Knyphausens were pinned against the creek and threw down their arms to St. Clair's brigade of Sullivan's division. The fighting was over in less than an hour. Rall was among the 22,948 taken prisoner, and four hundred others, including dragoons, escaped to the south. The Continentals took their prisoners, captured guns, and several wagonloads of booty back to their boats and recrossed the river.

Cadwallader assumed Washington had been hemmed in by the weather and wrote a message as such—only to find out a few hours later that Washington had indeed crossed the river. Embarrassed into belated action, Cadwallader crossed the river the next morning. Without orders, he proceeded to New Brunswick, which had been abandoned by the Hessians, and he proceeded to Crosswick. At that point, it finally dawned on Cadwallader to send a message to Washington.

That put Washington in a precarious position. If Cadwallader were left alone, he'd be overwhelmed by Cornwallis, who was on his way with 5,500 troops and another 2,500 already at Princeton. If Washington ordered his retreat, it would diminish their accomplishments achieved so far. Finally, if he were to order his men back across the river, it may discourage reenlistment and risk defeat at the hands of Cornwallis. As was his nature, Washington chose boldness and ordered his exhausted troops to cross the river again.

As Cornwallis marched through central New Jersey, some skillful delaying action slowed his advance. Washington managed 1,600 men to cross the river for the third time. He joined

Cadwallader in Trenton.

Expecting an attack from Cornwallis at any time, Washington skillfully evaded him by leaving a detachment to keep campfires while Washington took a little-known road east of Cornwallis's advance. He moved during the night to Cornwallis's rear and approached Princeton.

The British still occupied Princeton and Stony Brook Bridge, two miles south of town. A British brigade, headed by Colonel Charles Mawhood, had eight hundred men two of infantry and one cavalry and two guns.

The first to advance on the bridge was Mercer's brigade of Greene's division, and Mawhood immediately attacked. Washington, hearing fusillades, galloped to the scene and ordered Cadwallader to reinforce Mercer.

By that time, the British had attacked with bayonets and sent Mercer's men in retreat. Mercer was mortally wounded.

As Cadwallader's men saw Mercer's men retreating, they followed suit.

Washington rallied and shamed his men by advancing himself into the battle. He said, "Bring up the troops! Bring up the troops! The day is ours!" He reappeared unharmed. In a fifteen-minute battle, Mawhood had to use a bayonet charge to storm the bridge in retreat. Washington gave chase, but he rejoined Sullivan on his way into Princeton. British losses were more thana sixty killed and thirty-five prisoners. The Americans lost forty killed. At Princeton, the depot force was easily dispatched, taking another 115 prisoners. Washington allowed his troops pell-mell looting to find food, clothing, and shoes and put the rest to flame.

Washington proceeded to Morristown for winter quarters. After a miserable year of losses, the success of Trenton and Princeton redressed some of Washington's losses and his reputation, and it also provided a spark to reignite the Patriot cause.

JOANN

Joann Morrison's parents were very worried that their daughter had been missing for three ways and hadn't taken her clothes or any of her personal items. They called on a Detective Summers to try to find her. Summers headed straight to Morristown to find out where she had last been seen. He found several clothing stores that had sold her clothing, undergarments, and jewelry. He then got his first good lead by finding a restaurant owner who said she had visited him. He had taken her upstairs to his living quarters for food and beverages.

At first, Detective Summers suspected the man had abducted her or even killed her. However, he showed her where she had stored her clothes, jewelry, and dishes and silverware and then had taken the trunk and put it in a wagon headed for New York. The detective talked to a boy who had taken Joann to Princeton. As a Tory, she was headed for New York.

Joann and her friend Christine went shopping for dresses in Morristown. "Oh, Joann, that looks lovely on you!"

"Thanks, Christine. That is music to my ears. That's the fifth dress I've purchased; that should be enough for the trip."

"Let's go shopping for shoes."

Joann found some stylish heels and flats as well as walking boots and riding boots. They found a jewelry store and a china shop with dishes and silverware.

Joann and Christine went to a restaurant and went upstairs for dinner.

"I just love the things you bought, Joann. The undergarments are especially sexy!"

"Oh, thanks, Christine. That makes me especially happy coming from you, dear Christine. Well, we can spend one last night together before I leave in the morning for Princeton and then New York."

In the morning, Joann and Christine kissed each other goodbye, and Joann made her way to Princeton to meet her fiancé, Lieutenant James Stewart. Joann had hired a wagon to place her things, and the young wagoneer set off to Princeton. After rattling along for several miles, the boy decided to stop for some hay to support Joann's goods. They could hear some gunfire in the distance, and the boy said, "We better get going. If the Patriots find us, we're in big trouble. When we get to Princeton, it will be all Tories. We'll be safe there!"

The trip to Princeton went on without a hitch. Joann found a hotel, and the boy unloaded her things and wished her Godspeed. The next morning, Joann had breakfast, and her fiancé came to meet her at the hotel. They found an English Presbyterian Church and married in front of witnesses.

They honeymooned on the Jersey Shore, made their way to Harlem, and proceeded to his private officer's quarters. They set up housekeeping and hired some servants and a cook. Joann was very happy and planned for a child in the spring or early summer.

Detective Summers went to Princeton and spoke to an army officer who said Joann went with an officer to New York to get married. Surprised by this event, Summers had no choice but to try to track her down in New York. He finally located her in Harlem and asked her why she left home without a word. She told him that she didn't mean to scare her parents, but she knew she wouldn't be able to marry her lover without her parents' consent. She also said she couldn't send her parents a letter because it would jeopardize her and her new husband. He would have been tried for treason and executed, and she would have been tried as a spy and also executed.

After promising not to tell anyone, he said he would travel back to Morristown and let them know she was okay. Her parents were extremely grateful and said they would forgo any letters so as not to jeopardize Joann or her husband.

Joann did manage to send Christine a letter since they were both Tories. She told Christine the good news that she was pregnant and expecting in the late spring. Christine was delighted, and they kept in touch. On May 9, 1777, Joann gave birth to a baby girl and named her Tiffany. Joann and William were happily married, but William was a lieutenant in Cornwallis's army—and they ended up shipping out to Charleston, South Carolina.

After a little less than a year, Joann and Tiffany suddenly returned home. The parents were extremely grateful that they didn't have to worry about her anymore. She told them that she and her husband had parted on very good terms and would remain in touch as long as it didn't jeopardize his position in the army or his life. Her parents immediately arranged for an annulment of the marriage. Shortly after that, Joann and Tiffany moved in with Christine and seemed very happy. A happy and loving relationship between two women was known as a "Baltimore marriage."

William served well in Cornwallis's army in Charleston, Camden, Guilford Courthouse, and Yorktown. Then he found himself to be a prisoner of war and finally ended up in New York and disembarked back to England. Before he departed, he was able to meet his daughter and say goodbye to his wife. The promised to stay in touch and bade farewell. In England, he stayed in the army and ended up serving in India with Cornwallis.

BRANDYWINE

owe spent the early spring of 1777 inconclusively maneuvering against Washington in New Jersey. He finally withdrew his troops across the Hudson and back into New York. Washington knew that Burgoyne was headed to the Hudson via Lake Champlain, but what would Howe's next move be? It seemed to Washington that Howe would stay in New York and gradually move up the Hudson if Burgoyne needed help. Washington shifted his troops to central New Jersey and sent some of his best troops and commanders—including Morgan, Lincoln, and Arnold—to defend the Hudson. Howe made his move on July 23, sailing away with sixteen warships and 245 transports and supply ships.

Washington would have to wait to see if Howe really intended to strand Burgoyne by showing up on the Chesapeake headed for Philadelphia. When Howe showed up on September 1, Washington already had fifteen thousand troops waiting for him.

Washington's Continental troops consisted of five divisions commanded by Generals Greene, Sullivan, Stirling, and William Maxwell. Washington chose a position north of Wilmington on the east side of Brandywine Creek. He had some scouts reconnoiter the tributaries to the Brandywine River, but they failed to find the fordable places where Howe could cross the tributaries.

This was a major failing on Washington's part, and he should have reconnoitered the tributaries himself. He was on his own ground in a good defensive position, yet he allowed the British an advantage that could easily have been avoided. Washington had posted his divisions in good positions. Washington had deployed on cliffs overlooking Chadds Ford, Sullivan, Wayne, Maxwell, and Greene overlooking Chadds Ford. He had Maxwell in a forward position in front of Chadds Ford to cause a delaying action. He also had Bland's Dragoons west of Brandywine creek to divert any incursion. To the south, Armstrong held a position fortified in the cliffs above Pile's Ford.

The British decided to divide their army with Knyphausen continuing east and Howe and Cornwallis heading north on Great Valley Road. Sullivan posted Hazen to the northeast of the Brandywine, and Hazen was the first to report that Howe and Cornwallis were headed north on the Great Valley Road. This was surprising since Washington had not heard from Bland.

Washington ordered Bland to report, but it ended up being vague and unsatisfactory. Washington was convinced that Howe had divided his army, and he ordered Greene, Wayne, Maxwell, and Sullivan to cross the Brandywine and attack Knyphausen's division as part of attacking piecemeal. Before the attack, a farmer reported that Howe had crossed the Brandywine and was headed to the Birmingham Friends Meetinghouse.

Washington had to change his orders and place Sullivan farther north, facing Howe. He also ordered Stirling and Stephen to Sullivan's right. Those three divisions were just deploying when the British struck. General George Weedon of Greene's division arrived behind Sullivan's division.

At the same time, seeing the disorder, Knyphausen crossed the Brandywine for a frontal assault. The fighting with Cornwallis's division lasted about two hours until dark. At that point, Washington realized they had lost all their ground and good defensive positions, and he pulled his army back to Chester under the darkness of night.

The Americans had lost two hundred killed, seven to eight hundred wounded, and four hundred captured. The British reported eighty-nine killed, 488 wounded, and six missing. However, morale remained good for the American troops. Washington had made the mistake of relying on unreliable scouts to reconnoiter the Brandywine and lost his advantage of home ground and therefore lost the battle. Once again, Washington had to bear the responsibility.

Marnie

arnie was born in Philadelphia. Her father worked for a line of ships owned by her best friend's father. Marnie's father was a captain of the line of vessels out of Baltimore, and they headed out to an island known as Saint Eustatius, which recognized and gave a first salute to the flag of the United States of America. After Captain Peter Williams received the recognition from the island, they disembarked and settled on the island while the ship was unloaded.

The British had had enough of the independent island and decided to invade and conquer it for a good port of call and source of sugar and rum. Captain Williams was soon found out, and he was promptly executed. He was separated from his men and shot by a firing squad. The fleet was promptly confiscated, and the men reduced to slavery on board the British fleet. They were flogged for the slightest indiscretions.

The news traveled quickly to Joann and her mother, and they basically became wards of Joann's father. Joann lived in Baltimore during the school year and vacationed in Philadelphia, where she was befriended by Joann. During those summer years, Marnie also befriended James and their friend Philip. Philip was, like Joann, from

Morristown, and his father was also rich. As an adult, Marnie was a librarian and taught grade school. James was a farmer's son who had to go to school during the summers while the crops grew. Philip, Joann, Marnie, and James became friends.

When the British occupied Philadelphia, Joann and her mother were once again subjects of the Crown. Philip and James were part of Colonel Morgan's militia and took part in the Battle of Saratoga. Joann met Lieutenant Michael Loren and was encouraged by her mother to marry the officer. Joann was reluctant since she believed that she and James would marry someday. Joann's mother would have none of it and wanted her daughter married before her spinster years arrived— and that was very young in those days.

Joann reluctantly married Lieutenant Loren, and they decided to honeymoon in the Rittenhouse Square Hotel. This was when Joann got a shocking surprise. Lieutenant Loren told her he was homosexual and couldn't consummate the marriage. Even though Joann was well educated, she had never heard of homosexual behavior before. When she looked it up, it became clear that she and her mother had made a mistake. For Michael's part, getting married was a way to deflect his sexuality in the military's eyes and keep him from being executed. It appeared that it would be a short-lived marriage.

James received the shocking news and was clearly devastated. Philip was about to embark on a trip around the world, and James enrolled in the Continental Army, determined to shoot as many British officers as he could! James arrived just in time to winter in Valley Forge. His mettle would soon be tested, but he was determined to see his revenge through—no matter the futility of it. James survived the winter and was soon shaped into a professional military soldier by Von Steuben, Washington's drillmaster. He was ready for action, and he soon got his wish by being assigned to Horatio Gates's mission to Camden, South Carolina.

GERMANTOWN

Washington and Howe maneuvered against each other for a short period. At one point, Washington thought he could defeat the British as they came across the Schuylkill River, but the British only feinted and withdrew. The British easily marched into Philadelphia eight days later.

Howe then bivouacked in Germantown with eight thousand troops. He placed Cornwallis in Philadelphia and put another three thousand on the Delaware, helping the British fleet blockade the river. Howe prepared no defensive fortifications in Germantown.

On October 4, 1777, they launched a predawn attack on the British. Sullivan and Wayne attacked the British frontally, Armstrong attacked the British left, and Forman and Smallwood attacked the right flank. General Greene's guide lost his way and was almost an hour behind Sullivan's division. Nevertheless, he managed to push the British back into their camp. Washington, believing Greene was in fact in the British camp, thought a victory was at hand.

The battle was far from over, however. The British counterattacked Greene and drove him back. Continued mortar attacks on Chew House drew attention to both Stephen and Sullivan and Wayne's division to the rear.

Wayne's men ran out of ammunition, and then they and some of Greene's division began to break. Cornwallis was advancing from Philadelphia, and with his arrival, the left and right flank of the Patriots' attack failed. Realizing all hope was lost, Washington ordered a general withdrawal. The British lost seventy killed and 450 wounded, and the Americans lost 152 killed and 521 wounded. Morale was still high among the Americans since they believed they inflicted more casualties than they actually had.

SARATOGA

After the American disaster in the invasion of Canada and the surrender of Morgan, Burgoyne arrived on the scene to take over as first in command of the northern theater. Guy Carleton was to defend Canada, and Burgoyne would take the offensive on the Lake Champlain maneuver to control the Hudson Valley and divide the north colonies from the south ones. Burgoyne directed Frasier to proceed to St. Johns and then to the south end of Cumberland Bay at Point au Fer. Burgoyne had to go about a mile and a half to reach the tiny peninsula of Pointe au Sable. The invasion flotilla passed Ile aux Noix where a stockpile of barracks, magazines and powder awaited the army to launch the campaign. At that point, Burgoyne divided his army into three divisions. The Germans headed by Reidesel were to flank left to assault the eastern shore of the lake. The five hundred new Indians led by Frasier were to flank right ahead for scouting along with and to the rear General Phillips of the main right flank. Instead of the expected fifteen miles a day, the army only managed the mile and a half in a day and a half. Due to geography, the invasion would take very much longer!

Benedict Arnold awaited the fleet in his flotilla, expecting only to slow Burgoyne's advance and then disembark at Crown Pointe and then Fort Ticonderoga. As expected, Arnold's flotilla was no match for Burgoyne's fleet. He managed only a slight delaying action. However, that was not Burgoyne's main problem; he needed to have the land forces advance faster. The Indians with Phillips came up within a few days and scouted the Americans, but Reidesel would not be seen for days. As St. Clair surmised, the vanguard of the British Army declared in a letter to Schuyler: "No army was ever in a more critical situation than we now are." A general withdrawal to Fort Ticonderoga was in order.

At this point, a grave tactical error was made by the Americans. They reconnoitered Sugar Loaf Hill and Mount Defiance and decided it was too difficult for an army to drag artillery even though it was the highest point with a clear opening to shell Fort Ticonderoga. Burgoyne's engineers sent scouts ahead of Burgoyne and Phillips. They felt they could just manage to take the hill. So, while Burgoyne waited for Phillips to catch up, he sent ahead crews with artillery in hand to attempt the hill. It was a success, and when the troops came up, they could arm Mount Defiance.

Once again, the Americans had to mount a quick retreat. On the west side of the river was Fort Ticonderoga, and on the east side, most of the American army was on Rattlesnake Hill. The American flotilla on South Bay would head immediately to Skenesborough, basically giving up both Lake Champlain and Lake George. St. Clair had to get his army across to the east side and in full retreat to Fort Edwards.

At this point, the bad news from Schuyler had convinced Washington that a more experienced general, namely Horatio Gates, should defend the north. He also raised more militia and had one thousand men with Morgan and Tom Stark and the New Hampshire Grants. Another thousand could be expected; the Green Mountain Boys were already on the scene, retreating as the rear vanguard of the American defenses. These and the aroused Americans in the Northeast were piling in for admission.

Another big mistake for the British took place. A beautiful American redheaded woman was killed and scalped by the advanced Indian scouts, and the American became outraged. Everyone joined the defense.

Burgoyne finally cleared the forest before Fort Edward, but he still had to wait for his vanguard. Fort Edward was part of a pocket of forts along with Fort Anne, Fort George, and Fort Miller. As his troops slowly crossed, their scouts reconnoitered in Bennington. It was said they could retrieve some horses to supply the Germans' calvary they wanted. John Stark was waiting for them. As Reidesel advanced on Bennington, Stark intercepted them in a surprise attack. The result was a rout, and Reidesel had to retreat with what was left of his battered army. The forts had been entirely abandoned, and Gates lay entrenched just behind Saratoga.

One fort did hold, however, well to the west. The extreme right flank of Burgoyne's attack was headed by Lieutenant Colonel St. Ledger. Arnold had been sent by Schuyler to oppose St. Ledger. As Arnold advanced on Fort Stanwick, he found some men who had a mountaineer who was said to be half crazy. They instructed him to tell St. Ledger that he could not take the fort. St. Ledger decided to abandon the effort and come up on the rear of Burgoyne on Lake Champlain, which put him out of action for the remainder of the campaign.

At this point, the Indians had abandoned them. Burgoyne was at his weakest since the start of the campaign. With the sick and injured sent back to Lake Champlain, Burgoyne was now down two troops, but they were well-trained ones.

As Gates took over from Schuyler and the reinforcements came up, Gates now had nearly twelve thousand troops waiting for Burgoyne. Gates's troops were divided into five battalions. Morgan was at the extreme left to keep the British from flanking them. Dearborn was to his right, emplaced with Learned with Poor and Arnold on the right flank. Dearborn and Morgan worked well together and understood the difference between Continental troops who were good at marching and using muskets, much like the British and conventional European tactics, compared to the militia who liked to strafe and then melt back to reload. This was straight out of Israel Putnam's book on fighting in the American wilderness.

The Americans assumed that Burgoyne would not take the east side of the river because they would have to caissons on floats to attempt Albany. Burgoyne surmised, as the Americans anticipated, that he would need to take his right flank, which took him directly at Morgan. The British left flank headed close to the river, straight toward the redoubts that were built by Thaddeus Kosciusko, a Polish engineer working with the Americans. It was nearly impregnable, and it also served as Gates's headquarters.

Morgan had hidden his troops behind an overgrown fence line and placed a large number of men in bushes and trees. The British fought with muskets that were notoriously inaccurate. Morgan's men had long guns that only the militia carried. The muskets had the advantage of quick reload every fifteen seconds, but the long guns took a full minute. The muskets also had bayonets that could not be mounted on long guns.

The Americans also had the advantage of being used to hunting. They were sharpshooters, and the British were terrible shots with inaccurate weapons. As the British marched down a steep hill, they felt like they were being watched. At less than one hundred feet, the Americans opened fire. The deadly volley put the British just where they wanted them—straight on their center with Dearborn and Learned waiting to fire.

Most of the fighting took place in a wheat field the British had retreated to and were easy pickings as Learned's men marched into them. Morgan had finally regathered his men with a turkey whistle and pounded again at the British right flank. As the Americans came on them at the wheat field—and Learned continued forward—the

British again had to retreat to a fenced-over area with cover. Poor's men were also advancing on the British left flank.

Benedict Arnold came charging on a horse with a cavalry unit. Gates and Arnold had been at loggerheads since Gates arrived. Arnold was ordered out of action, but the other commanders overruled Gates. Arnold was said to take some ladles of rum and mount a horse to lead the cavalry into the breach. He came just in time to assault the British astride the fence cover they had taken. He proceeded to rout them. Ruisdael was too close to the river to be of any help for Burgoyne. As the remaining American forces came up the British were forced to skedaddle back toward Saratoga to camp.

For three days, the two forces reconnoitered their respective positions. Burgoyne began a redoubt just short of Saratoga. John Stark had fled the scene as his troops had reached their release from duty. The first attack came again from the American left flank that Morgan had reassembled. It was a first line assault on the British right redoubt. Arnold attacked the center with the remaining troops shifted right to cut off any escape down the Hudson.

In the meantime, Stark had gotten reenlistments, returned to the field, and cut off Burgoyne to the north if he attempted to retreat back to Lake Champlain. As the troops attacked the redoubts, American artillery was pounding the rear. Night fell, and then it rained most of the night. The British convened counsel and decided to surrender. They started their offensive in May, and it was October. For months, they had been operating under terrible geological conditions and diseases spreading through the troops and constantly moving forward and barely resting. The weather was against them in the end. They were a completely spent force at the end of the operation.

The British surrendered about seven thousand soldiers, and they were to be sent to Boston. The American Army reversed itself and decided to send the captives south after they were partway across Massachusetts. They would be captives for the remainder of the war. They also lost a great officer, Frazier, who was shot on the second day of the American assault on the British redoubt. He died on the last day of surrender.

Gates would take first credit since Burgoyne surrendered to him. Later, Arnold was given the most credit for winning the surrender. Both strategically and tactically, Morgan was the true reason for such an aggressive offensive and defensive position, and he deserves the credit for leading the entire offensive against the British right flank. Morgan was always the first attack at both Freeman's farm and at the final British redoubt.

After Burgoyne surrendered, he went to Albany with most of the staff and wives and children and had dinner with Schuyler before he left for New York City and went back to London.

FAITH

The next morning, they got their shopping list for Colonel Morgan's party, hitched the horses to their wagon, and proceeded to the store. On the way to the store, they ran into Running Bear. He was the first son of Big Bear, the medicine man for the Pennsylvania Mohican Tribes. Running Bear kept running as usual and ran alongside the wagon.

When they got to the store, they took out their shopping lists and began picking out things. They purchased wheat and corn flour, chicken and beef, lots of fruits and vegetables, and some whiskey, rum, wine, port, and beer. They loaded their wagon and started toward home. Running Bear took off toward his wagon and traded venison and fish for grain, vegetables, and fruit and some beer, whiskey, rum, and wine. He would go to the Cumberland Gap where his uncle, Great Red Bear, was the medicine man for the Mohican Tribe in Kentucky. All medicine men were named Bear.

Running Bear used the road that was first blazed by Colonel Morgan, "the old wagon master." It went straight from Virginia to Kentucky. Colonel Morgan had also used a road that went from Maryland to Pennsylvania to supply Washington's force, attached to the British in the French and Indian Wars, with food and military supplies. Running Bear proceeded to the Cumberland Gap and helped unload the wagon for his uncle Great Red Bear. Living up to his name, Running Bear then ran back to Pennsylvania Trail and then headed west for home and arrived in just two days. His father, family, and friends welcomed him home.

Faith was born a slave. She was born in the masters' house along with her two brothers. In Virginia and elsewhere on southern plantations, the slave owners looked upon the slaves as a breeding ground—so the more children of slaves, the better. It was viewed in the same way as livestock of which they were considered as such.

Faith's mother worked in the big house as a maid and so lived a better life. To free her mother up for her domestic duties, Faith and her brothers were put into the home school. They weren't really meant to learn as much as it was generally thought by slave owners that they were incapable of advanced learning. Ah, but here was an exception. Faith was extremely bright. She was intellectually far brighter than her master's children. From an early age, she mastered all subjects and was particularly exceptional at math and science. So, here was an unusual situation where the slave labor expected was rather an intellectual asset instead. Under normal circumstances, this would have been ignored.

Perhaps because of their privileged situation within the community or just a more enlightened view of these particular plantation owners, Faith's gifts were recognized by nearly everyone early on, and the master was not immune to utilizing this resource. Faith's two brothers would be put in the fields as soon as they were old enough

"Father and Mother have invited Colonel Morgan to the big dance, and she wants you to serve punch of course. Of course. Your father has asked me to do the math of conversion from tobacco to wheat. Unfortunately, there is nothing I can do to help him since the British paid regardless of the debt. At least it was something. Trying to sell wheat into worthless paper that is a black market is a losing proposition no matter what. It's better than nothing I suppose." "Faith, what are you going on about?"

The plantation was relatively small with just thirty-five or so slaves. It wasn't good business to split up families, so this was several extended families. Thomas and Rachael Stevens had three children: Paul, Michael, and Lauren. Paul and Michael were old enough to oversee the fields and the work crews. Lauren was expected to help her mother with domestic work and social planning. She adopted Faith as things went so well with her around. Her father, like many plantation owners, was trying to preserve capital and badly needed management in perfect order. Faith provided bookkeeping and asset management as well.

Being in debt to the British was now almost inconsequential, but with the embargo, tobacco had declined in value. Only smuggling to France and Belgium was still a market at all. Wheat was a universal commodity, and it always had value—even in heavily devalued Continental paper. It was in customhouses that any exchange of goods determined their value. Thomas was in constant fear of bankruptcy due to lost commodity value. The war could not continue without the privateers smuggling that kept the planters in business at all.

To make matters worse, this was a time of British raiding parties, including Benedict Arnold. The farms were ripe pickings, but burning fields was an arduous task—so raider damage was generally limited. Virginia was the heart and soul of the revolution, but it never actually experienced much war. As hard as it was to occupy cities in friendly territory, occupying countryside was simply out of the question, which Cornwallis would soon learn in the Carolinas.

Faith's mother, Bell, worked in the master's kitchen, but she was also expected to do any domestic chores she was able to do. Her father, Albert, was a strong man and well suited to domestic life, and he worked the fields. He was in charge of some of the field work. One of his distant relatives, a single man named Joseph, had manners and such to fill manly servant duties as a butler and the master's attendant.

Albert didn't have time or presence at the house, so a natural tension arose between Albert and Thomas in terms of jealousy on Albert's part and guilt for Thomas.

For this big dance, Thomas would have to train Albert for all hands on deck on the biggest occasion during the entire plantation's life. Although this was a strain for Albert, it wasn't nearly as bad as keeping Master Paul at bay. Paul was overseeing Albert's area since it was the biggest and most productive. Paul, however, had a mean streak that was only kept at bay by his father and the diligence of Albert. Whippings did not increase production, but Paul didn't handle stress well—and punishment would result. Michael, on the other hand, despised his brother and his bullying ways as he had experienced as a child. So, the intrigue was all about catering to Paul's needs to prevent mishaps that led to whippings.

Faith was with her grandmother, her mother, and her parents' best friend, the butler Thomas. They were cooking dinner, which was chicken, mashed potatoes, corn on the cob coleslaw, and Dutch apple pie for dessert, which was made by Faith's grandmother. When everything was nearly ready, one of the field slaves under Thomas came running up saying that

Paul had whipped Albert one hundred times, and he was bleeding badly. Bell ran out to help Thomas and brought him in with his arm on her shoulder. They sat Albert down, and though they could not bandage his back, they applied alcohol to keep him from getting infected. He would have to sleep on his stomach. They finished dinner, and when they began to serve it, Bell overheard Michael explaining the beating administered by his brother Paul on Albert. The Stevens were outraged. Then they found out Paul, who knew he was in trouble, had fled the plantation and was headed to Pennsylvania to join Washington's Continental Army.

For the next week, the Stevens and their slaves prepared for a big party they were putting on for Colonel Morgan. He was just back from Saratoga after his big victory, and he was retiring. They were brewing some beer and distilling some whiskey. They also began to prepare the food that they could. Faith's grandmother, Opra, was preparing apple, strawberry, and lemon pies. Bell was preparing canned goods, such as beans, tomatoes, tomato hot salsa, corn, and peaches. Faith was in charge of preparing bread dough that would be placed in the dry room with Grandma Opra's pies.

Albert had not healed, but he returned to the fields after just two days of rest. It was late fall, and they had to harvest the crops or lose them. While he was underfoot with Bell and their friend Thomas, he became suspicious of the relationship between Bell and Thomas. It was eating away at him as he went back to the fields.

So, the big day came for Colonel Morgan's victory party. They had prepared baked ham, spareribs, baked potatoes, and yams. They made a big salad with spinach, mushrooms, tomatoes, red, yellow, and green peppers, onions, and hot peppers. Bell's canned goods were served as side dishes. Faith's bread was baked and served with the main course. Grandma Opra's pies were baked and kept in the dry room to retain their heat.

All the neighbor farmers with their entourages were there ready to eat and dance. As Colonel Morgan arrived, he looked over at Albert and noticed something wrong right away. It looked like his back was bleeding. "Did something tawdry happen to you, son? It looks like you were whipped? I know I got four hundred lashes when I was a wagoneer. I hit a British officer and was convicted of insubordination even though I didn't belong to their army. I didn't think Master Stevens allowed that? You can tell me. I won't tell anyone else." "No, sir," Albert replied. "Master Stevens don't allow no whippins. His son Paul got his head up about the yield. He thought we were niggardly in our duties, but we was right on schedule. Honest, Colonel Morgan.

"I believe you, Albert.

"Paul had a mind, and he moved on, sir. He went to join General Washington's Continental in Pennsylvania."

"I'm sure His Excellency, General Washington, will take good care of him. I'll send some salve that will help your back tomorrow." The colonel moved on to pay his respects to the other families.

Thomas couldn't help but notice a beautiful maid with Colonel Morgan's entourage. Her name was Virginia, and she was the most beautiful woman Thomas ever encountered. There was the white man's dance floor and a Negro dance floor set up behind the orchestra. A lot of the families did not believe in this arrangement, but Colonel Morgan thought it was a good idea, and the rest went along with it. Thomas saw his opportunity and went for it. He asked Virginia for a dance, and it was love at first sight. They only had one dance together since they both had to get back to their respective duties.

The next morning, as promised, Colonel Morgan sent over the salve for Albert's back. He sent Virginia, and it gave Thomas an opportunity to ask her to go for a walk later in the week. She was ecstatic and agreed for him to come pick her up. Since Thomas was the chauffeur as well as the butler, he was allowed to take the carriage and pick her up. Virginia was waiting, and they had a scenic ride in the country. They also stopped off to go for a walk in a park.

Thomas didn't have a ring, but he offered Virginia his hand in marriage. She was delighted. Thomas had to tell her he was about to join the Continental Army and wanted to wait until his service was up.

Virginia was disappointed but mostly afraid of him serving in the army and getting killed. "Godspeed, dear Thomas, come back to me alive, safe, and unharmed," she exclaimed through her tears.

"Virginia, I have everything to live for. I will be back—and we'll spend the rest of our lives together."

Early's Advice

"Where's my men?" General Morgan asked.

Just then, Early appeared.

"Where the hell did you come from, Early?"

"I just came to give you some advice, General Morgan," replied Early.

"Okay, let's have it," continued General Morgan.

"Why don't you use your turkey whistle to find where they're hiding." Morgan used his whistle, and his men appeared from behind the trees, bushes, and split-rail fences. "Wow! That's great, Early."

Early vanished in a cloud of sparkling stars.

"I know what you're thinking, Early. Don't even think about it—or you'll get a devil of a whipping!"

After Philip Brady fought bravely with his friend James and Colonel Morgan and the militia, he decided he had had enough of war. Since it was virtually won with the surrender of Burgoyne and the French joining the cause, he decided to travel around the world. With his parents' approval and funding, he set sail to his first stop in Mexico. He was, indeed, a lucky man

Around the World and the Seven Seas

Philip Brady's first stop was Veracruz, Mexico. He would sail up the Tecolutla River and would join Christiana Santi, the famous Argentinian soprano and Johan Betts from Germany in Veracruz. From there, they would proceed by horseback to Mexico City. Since Philip's father was paying for it, the party had three serf servants to attend to their needs.

At one point, Philip's horse encountered a rattlesnake and nearly bucked him off. Fortunately, Christina was able to come along broadside and keep him safe. Christiana also managed to shoot the snake with her handgun. Christiana and Johann had been together for several years, but they had split up some months ago. They remained together to get paid for the trip by Philip's father. Johan was largely useless, but they needed the extra money. Christiana saved Philip's life more than once on the trip. She even managed to save their baggage when it was tipped over in the boat that Johan rocked. Philip and Christiana spent their nights together in their tent for a mutually accepted good time. After they reached Mexico City, they boarded river rafts to float to the Pacific.

Along the way, Christiana sang Mozart's "Magic Flute," which was all the rage throughout Europe at the time. Mozart was all the rage in the late seventeenth century. German beer garden music, polka, was popular during Johann Strauss's time, and he and his sons wrote a lot of the popular music of the time. Johann Strauss II later turned the popular polka music into beautifully composed songs such as "The Blue Danube" and "Tales from the Vienna Woods." His operettas included *Die Fledermaus, The Gypsy Baron, A Night in Venice,* and *Cinderella.* Johann Strauss II composed more than five hundred waltzes, polkas, quadrilles, marches, mazurkas, and gallops.

In Mexico, German beer brewers introduced polka to the Mexican people. The music was so popular it became Mexico's national musical heritage. Later, the music evolved into what's known today as either *norteño* or *banda.*

The Bourbon kings in Spain decided not to divide Mexico, the Philippines, and the West Indies into two administrative units as they did with Peru. The first administration was headed by Jose de Galvez. He became the first Commandancy General of the Internal Provinces of the North (*Comandancia y Capitanía General de las Provincias Interna*). He made Theodore de Croix commander general of the *Provinicas Internas*, independent of the viceroy. This included Nueva Vizcaya, Nuevo Santander, Sonora and Sinaloa, las Californias, Coahuila and Tejas (Coahuila and Texas), and Nuevo México.

As Philip made his way to the Philippines, Christiana and Johann sailed to the Isthmus of Panama. Johann went back to Germany, and Christiana went back to resume her operatic career in Argentina.

FAITH

When Benedict Arnold, the traitor, and his British force came through the Virginia countryside, most of the farmers fled. Faith was in contact with all the slaves on the plantation south of Colonel Morgan's plantation. Since the plantation owners had fled ahead of Arnold's army, the slaves were, in essence, free. They were ecstatic about their newfound freedom—as anyone would be.

The most important part, however, was getting their wives away from the plantation since the owner and his sons routinely raped their women. Faith went to Colonel Morgan's to find a route for their flight to a free life. Morgan knew what she was up to, but he immediately dismissed it from his mind since he disliked his neighbor and his cruel ways. She would take them on the Pennsylvania road that Morgan had blazed all the way to eastern Ohio. The family never returned to central Virginia and had to accept a buyer's offer that didn't include their slaves since they would never return to look for them.

Faith left them there, and they had to start from scratch. That suited them just fine since they were free at last. Although few visitors came by, they still had to make their dwellings somewhat stealthy. They made a fake plantation house where they shared kitchen privileges with rooms for the older children. The fake plantation was then cleared of trees, and crops were planted on the hundred-acre plot. Out on each of the four corners, slave quarters were built. Each cabin had plenty of acreage for more crops and livestock. All of this was designed to prevent people who passed by from thinking they were runaways. As it happened, no one ever bothered them. As the community grew, a township was started—and the former slaves now lived just like everyone else.

Daniel Morgan

After Morgan had his victory party, he and his wife went back to their plantation. One of the reasons he didn't whip his slaves was that he had been given a hundred lashes after punching a British officer during the French and Indian War—even though he wasn't even part of their army. He had left home at an early age and settled in Virginia. He was often in fights with the local ruffians and won all the fights. He did, however, have one foe who gave him trouble. He was a tall, thin redhead. On one occasion, the redhead had jumped on Morgan's back, which caused him sciatica for the rest of his life.

During the French and Indian War, he carried wagon supplies to Washington's troops. He was called the "Old Wagoneer."

On the first outing, Washington's men had been shot at by a few Indian scouts—and they started firing at each other. It was foggy, and they didn't know who they were firing at. Washington soon realized the debacle and interceded, risking his own life. Morgan became well acquainted with Washington, and Washington liked his muster.

Daniel Morgan is believed to have been born in the village of New Hampton, New Jersey, in Lebanon Township. All four of his grandparents were Welsh immigrants who lived in Pennsylvania.

Morgan was the fifth of seven children of James Morgan (1702–1782) and Eleanor Lloyd (1706–1748). When Morgan was seventeen, he left home following a fight with his father. After working at odd jobs in Pennsylvania, he moved to the Shenandoah Valley. He finally settled on the Virginia frontier, near what is now Winchester, Virginia.

He worked clearing land, in a sawmill, and as a teamster. In just a year, he saved enough to buy his own team. Morgan had served as a civilian teamster during the French and Indian War with his cousin Daniel Boone. After returning from the advance on Fort Duquesne (Pittsburgh) by General Braddock's command, he was punished with 499 lashes (a usually fatal sentence) for striking his superior officer. Morgan thus acquired a hatred for the British Army. He then met Abigail Curry; they married and had two daughters, Nancy and Betsy.

Morgan later served as a rifleman in the provincial forces assigned to protect the western settlements from French-backed Indian raids. After the war, he purchased a farm near Winchester, Virginia. By 1774, he was so prosperous that he owned ten slaves. That year, he served in Dunmore's War, taking part in raids on Shawnee villages in the Ohio Valley Country. He forever hated the British after the French and Indian War, and he vowed to get even. He always said that they were one short on their lashes and owed him one. He took possession of that owed one by routing the British and Tarleton at Cowpens.

Monmouth Courthouse

After a miserable winter at Valley Forge, a remarkable recovery instigated by von Steuben's manual of muskets and marching regimen gave new hope for the fighting prowess of the Americans. General Howe had been sent home. General Clinton replaced Howe and was ordered to evacuate Philadelphia back to New York. Clinton chose the land route.

The British plans for 1778 changed and now aimed at the Southern Colonies. They had to evacuate Philadelphia first. Washington now had 14,500 well-trained troops thanks to von Steuben to Clinton's sixteen thousand. Washington put an advanced guard of two thousand troops in Lafayette's hands. He was to pursue Clinton as they left Philadelphia.

The British crossed the Delaware, and Lafayette took off ahead of him. The remainder of Washington's army followed. Washington's army waited while Clinton made his way to Monmouth. After they arrived, the British rested out of the hot sun.

At this point, Washington ordered General Lee to attack and told him the rest of the army would come to reinforce him. Lee issued no orders, but he started a slow advance to Monmouth. Some of the advanced guards attacked, and others simply stopped in the broiling sun. Clinton ordered Cornwallis to counterattack. The Americans broke and ran—with the exception of Wayne's brigade who withdrew in good order.

Washington was disturbed by the sparse sounds of battle and moved forward to investigate. He was highly disappointed to see fleeing troops. Then he came upon Lee and said, "What, sir, is the meaning of this? Whence does the disorder and confusion come from?" He moved further on and found Wayne's brigade out in front of the British by about two hundred yards. Washington began rounding up Lee's stragglers. He found a low ridge overlooking a shallow depression and made a stand. Washington's cool presence and determined leadership were the difference between a rout and a successful stand.

The Americans had 350 deaths, forty from heatstroke. The British 358 deaths, including fifty-nine from sunstroke. At midnight, the British broke camp and marched to Sandy Hook to awaiting ships. After the battle, Lee offered no explanation or excuses and asked for a court-martial and an apology from Washington. Instead, he received a suspension from his command as well as dismissal from the army. This time, the debacle could not be blamed on Washington. The Americans could also look to the success of Von Steuben's shaping up of the army.

Savannah, Georgia

Sir Henry Clinton, starting his campaign in the south, started by sending Lieutenant Colonel Archibald Campbell to Savannah, Georgia. Campbell disembarked at the mouth of the Savannah River, thirty miles southwest of the city. Major General Robert Howe had about a thousand Patriot soldiers to check Campbell's advance. Campbell used a double envelopment and shattered the Patriot troops. The Americans lost eighty-three killed and 433 captured. The British lost only three men killed and eighteen wounded. Major General Augustine Prevost, commanding British troops in East Florida, marched with a small force into Georgia and captured Fort Sunbury and then continued on and joined Campbell in Savannah.

French Admiral d'Estaing accepted an invitation from Governor Rutledge and General Moultrie in Charleston to help capture Savannah. Major General Benjamin Lincoln was in command of the Southern Patriot forces with a thousand Continentals and 1,500 militiamen and proceeded from Charleston to Savannah. He came to the Savannah River on its east bank, just north of Savannah. Prevost had only 2,500 troops, including slaves, Tories, and a Hessian detachment. With a total of 1,350 American troops under Lincoln and another five thousand French troops under Admiral 'Estaing, these forces attacked on September 16. Pulaski attacked charging head-on into the British middle against entrenchments. He was killed, and his troops scattered. D'Estaing attacked from the left and was repulsed at Sailor's Battery. Lincoln's Continentals and the main French infantry pierced the main British defenses near Spring Hill, but after an hour of fighting, they were also repulsed and had to retire.

The allies lost 244 killed and 584 wounded. The British reported forty killed, sixty-three wounded, and sixty-two missing. Savannah survived and remained in British hands. The battle lasted nine more days and ended with d'Estaing re-embarking with his troops, sailing off on October 20. Lincoln retired north of the Savannah River before returning to Charleston. The Savannah operations were a dismal failure for the Americans and their French allies.

Around the World and the Seven Seas

Philip entered Manila, Philippines, looking forward to some song, dance, drink, and women. While he was dancing, he met a beautiful young woman. She took him to her room and made love to him. After he paid her the next morning, he decided to see the city. It was no less than a tropical paradise. He then found a cafe and had a nice cup of tea. He also imbibed in snorting some lines of cocaine and then walked it off by taking a nighttime walk. The next morning, he checked with his father's bank and started planning his next trip to China.

The next morning, Philip decided to go coral diving. He met with his ship's owner, Miguel, and they proceeded out to the nearest coral reef. After diving, Miguel came up first with a nice large coral, and Philip followed with his.

Miguel said, "That was a nice dive, and we have two beautiful large coral to show for it." They proceeded to do five more dives and then went back to shore.

Philip paid Miguel with a generous bonus and also gave him his coral, which would fetch a nice price at the Manila farmers market.

Philip went back to his hotel and had a dinner of lobster, baked potato, and key lime pie. He also drank several margaritas and then went up to his room to prepare for his trip to China. The next morning, he embarked on a Spanish vessel and proceeded to sail to China.

During the eighteenth century, the Philippines was mostly under the colonial rule of the Spanish. There were, however, different ruling systems and colonial rulers. The Spanish quickly introduced a feudal type of colonial rule. They first used reduction or relocation of the native Filipinos. Conquistadores, noble friars, and native nobles were granted estates. Military protection was provided by the estates through the king against the French, the Dutch, the Chinese, and pirates.

Charles III (1759–1788) appointed a Council of the Indies that governed through his representative, the governor-general of the Philippines. Jose de Basco y Vegas was the governor-general from 1733 to 1805. He had control of the army, the navy, and all economic planning of the country. He also controlled the ecclesiastic appointments and local government. Agriculture was still their main form of trade and income. He founded the Royal Order of Economic Society and Friends of the Country. This resulted in the establishment of the Silversmiths, Gold Beaters Guild, and the first paper mill.

King Charles also established the Royal Philippine Company, which was the trading company for the Philippines. It brought Chinese and Indian goods in and exported, around the Cape of Good Hope, goods from the Philippines to Europe. It also had a monopoly on Venezuelan trade. Taxation was exercised by both tributes from rice and forty days of labor (later reduced to fifteen) rendered for the government.

The first attacks came from the Dutch but were limited to the village of Lindao. However, Dutch assistance and aid never appeared, and the invasion failed to materialize. The next attack came from the British during the Seven Years War between the British and the allied French, Dutch, and Spanish. They succeeded in capturing Manila but then stalled out and stayed put. The Spanish and Filipino troops kept the British confined to Manila. The British kept hopes alive after receiving a surrender from the Catholic archbishop, Rojo, in October 1762.

Governor-General Salazar rejected the surrender. He kept the British confined to Manila and crushed British fomented revolts. He also blockaded any trade from Manila. The Seven Years War ended with the Treaty of Paris, which was signed on February 10, 1763. There was no mention of Manila specifically in the treaty, but the general provision provided the return of Manila to the Spanish. After the Seven Years War, resistance to the Spanish mostly from the Filipino Nobles, continued but was largely unsuccessful.

Under the rule of Governor-General Basco, trade was opened up and flourished. They exported sugar, hemp, Negroes, and tobacco. The Jesuits made all the trade and prosperity possible. Although the European governments were jealous and suspicious of the Jesuits, they acted not just as a religious order; they had educators, scientists, geographers, and financiers who brought them wealth and power—not that different from the other colonialists. They were an international organization that was not loyal to any one state or country. They were not patriots. Near the end of the eighteenth century, they were dissolved or expelled from most European countries. They were finally expelled from the Philippines in 1767. The Philippine government seized their property, which amounted to 1,350,000 pesos.

Governor Don Simon de Anda returned to power in 1770 and was bitterly opposed by the Friars. He fought long and hard against the friars' corruption or any corruption at all. He was, himself, not corruptible. He fought an uphill battle and had little support or means, but in his six years in power, he had some limited success.

The final assault of Spanish control came from a group of pirates called the Moros. In 1771, they attacked Aparri in the far northern corner of Luzon and captured a Spanish mission. Toward the end of his rule, Anda reorganized the Armada de Pintados and built a fleet of gunships to attack the Moros. The English evacuated Manila. With a treaty, the Moros secured the Island of Balanbangan off the northern coast of Borneo. The Moros then attacked the British with great fury and destroyed an entire garrison.

The Spanish rule of the Philippines provided a general upgrade in agriculture and industry that resulted in export and trade that was very lucrative. Governor-General Anda died in October 1776, but he was not succeeded until July 1778 by Don Jose Basco de Vargas. His "Plan General Economico" continued the expansion of growth in agriculture and industry and started the growing of cotton and cultivating silkworms in Mulberry bushes. He also expanded tobacco growth and made it highly profitable to the extent that they no longer depended on Mexico for financial support.

CHARLESTON, SOUTH CAROLINA

After learning the siege of Savannah had failed, Clinton decided to embark to Charleston, South Carolina, with 8,500 troops, leaving General Knyphausen with the same amount of troops in New York. Clinton learned on his way to Charleston that the allied siege of Savannah had failed. The British troops disembarked on Johns Island, thirty miles south of Charleston. General Lincoln began fortifying Charleston with a thousand troops. General Clinton slowly marched to the Ashley River, south of Charleston, and then pushed his troops north of the city to begin a siege.

On the same day, the British fleet sailed into the harbor, easily passing a savage cannon fire from two forts. On April 10, Clinton and Admiral Arbuthnot asked Lincoln for a general surrender. Lincoln refused, and the British began their siege on April 13. On the same day, a force of infantry and cavalry were able to block Lincoln's communication along the Cooper River line.

General Lincoln and his war council decided to escape the city to the east south of Tarleton across the Cooper River. The city fathers attended the council and threatened to destroy the river boats if Lincoln attempted to escape through the swamps. Lincoln weakly caved in and stayed in the city. Clinton declined Lincoln's suggestion to evacuate the city with full honors of war. The British manned their siege lines and prepared to attack so Clinton again suggested surrender, but Lincoln wanted full honors of war that Clinton promptly refused. On May 9, hostilities resumed. An artillery battle lasted all night, and Lincoln finally had to agree to a general surrender.

Patriot losses were one hundred killed and 150 wounded. The British losses were seventy-six killed and 189 wounded. When the British saw how few troops defended the city, they praised the Americans for their gallant defense. Clinton proceeded to occupy the city on May 18.

CAMDEN

T he battle north of Camden on the border European army marching in columns across flat countryside with sparse cover to pound the enemy before them. British assumptions of the reconquest of all of South Carolina proved to be premature. General Gates showed his true fighting tactics were a complete disaster. It could probably be said the Gates completely disgraced himself and probably should have been relieved of duty. He may even be accused of cowardice.

Most of the militia immediately broke ranks and fled. Only a few Continentals held their ground—only to be flanked by units who routed the militias. After initially confronting the British centerline, General de Kalb's forces drove the British back to their original line. The British counterattacks drove the Patriots off the field. General de Kalb's horse was shot out from under him, and he was shot eleven times. Cornwallis ordered the giant hero to be taken to British doctors, but after two hours, he succumbed to his wounds. British casualties were seventy-nine dead and 245 wounded. American casualties were six hundred dead and one thousand captured.

Gates proceeded to retreat sixty miles to Charlotte, North Carolina, and by the second night, he'd gone 180 miles to Hillsboro.

Afterward, Hamilton sarcastically wrote, "180 miles in three and a half days. It does admiral credit to the activity of a man at this time of his life." For the Patriots, it was truly a case of the darkest hour being just before dawn.

AROUND THE WORLD AND THE SEVEN SEAS

Philip found, in China, a very peaceful nation. King Jeongjo had taken over rule after his grandfather died in 1776. Philip found a suitable hotel on his first night. He had a nice meal of Peking duck, rice, noodles, and a sweet Chinese tea. Afterward, he found the bar and had a great brew ale. Philip asked the bartender, "Where do you get your excellent beer?"

Mai Tong said, "We get them from two different sources; they are rival gangs in competition with each other—so we have to buy from both to keep them from killing each other." Mai Tong explained that his son was in one of the gangs, but to keep the peace, he bought from both sources.

Mai Tong's daughter came in the bar. Seng Sou was a beautiful young woman of about twenty-two. "Father, has Chin Lee come in yet?"

Her father replied, "He did, but he said he had more customers on his route." Weng Sou and Chin Lee were an item and an item of contention since they were from rival gang families. It was sort of a Romeo and Juliet saga.

After a while, Mai Tong asked Philip if he would like to liaison to the rival gang for him since he wanted to make peace. "You have to be careful not to mention my daughter and her boyfriend since that will worsen the conflict and possibly end up dead."

Philip agreed to approach the rival gang since he would be seen as neutral. Philip went to bed feeling like he might be able to do some good and possibly resolve the conflict. Philip awoke in the morning and went to the hotel restaurant for an early meal. He had hot tea egg foo young with rice and noodles and a large piece of ham.

In the bar, Mai Tong said, "My daughter's boyfriend, Chin Lee, will take you to the Quin gang to open negotiations."

When Philip and Chin arrived, the gang leaders were talking about the possibility of another gang war if they couldn't expand their base of operations. Philip was introduced as a neutral mediator who could appeal to the Seajong gang to allow the Quins into previously forbidden territories. Temporarily satisfied their desires could possibly be met, they called off the conference and gave Philip a list of their demands.

Philip returned to the hotel and appraised Mai Tong of his meeting with the Quins. Mai Tong told Philip he would convey his message to the Seajongs and let him know what the decision was tomorrow. He also told Philip that he could go back to the Quins with Chin Lee after Chin completed his beer rounds.

Philip went to dinner and had hot tea, Kung Pao chicken with hot pepper sauce and rice and noodles, and a large cilantro salad with lentils, tomatoes, red, green, and yellow peppers, and chicken slices covered with a hot pepper sauce and sour cream. After this hot food, Philip decided to go back to the bar for some more beer. While he was there, he witnessed the loving relationship between Weng Sou and Chin Lee, and he was touched by the affection they displayed. He had a bad premonition, however, that he tried to erase from his thoughts that trouble would brew with this relationship.

The next morning, after breakfast, Philip received the excellent news that the Seajongs had accepted the Quins' proposals without other stipulations or reservations. He had his lunch of hot tea, charcoaled pork, beef, and chicken wraps with pork chops, and flan. Later in the afternoon, Philip joined Chin Lee and went to the Chins with acceptance of new territories for the Quins. There was cause for celebration.

Just as peace seem to be restored, Chin Lee's parents dressed him down about his relationship. He was mortified. The Chin leadership overheard the dressing down of Chin Lee by his parents and warned Chin against any such relationship. This breach of propriety between the gangs was not allowed. Philip and Chin returned to the hotel bar. Just as Chin was relaying the bad news to Weng Sou, her brother arrived. He was mortified that his sister would even think of getting involved with Chin Lee. The two lovers left with a cloud of sorrow over their heads.

The next morning, Philip arose to the bad news that Weng and Chin had committed suicide in a lover's embrace. Weng's father was in a state of shock. He dressed down his son's interference, and his son wept for hours. Philip had to take the sorrowful news to the Quins and Chin's parents. It was received equally badly by the Quins and Chin's parents. After these sorrowful events, the two gangs vowed to end hostilities—and the parents of the two lovers forbade any further hostilities.

By 1780, China was a peaceful nation governed by the Yeongion Regime, which was part of the Qing Regime, was the last Imperial Dynasty that lasted from 1644 to 1911 (King Yeongio from 1724 to 1776 and his grandson Jeongio from 1776 to 1800). The two kings reformed the tax system, which grew the revenue stream into the treasury, strengthened the military, sponsored a revival of learning, started a printing press using movable type, and sharply increased publication. Jeongio sponsored scholars from various parts of the country.

In the middle of the nineteenth century, two factions of Muslims began fighting. The Japanese Samurai invaded but were later thwarted by the Chinese military. The two disparate Muslim groups joined together and attacked China. They were thwarted in their efforts, which proved to be catalyst for most of the reforms in the overseas possessions, just like the War of the Spanish Succession had been for the reforms on the peninsula. By the end of Qianlong emperor's long reign in 1796, the Qing Empire was at its zenith. While the Qing dynasty ruled, they were the largest economy in the world.

The Qing Dynasty (1644–1911) was the last imperial dynasty in China. Founded by the Manchus, it was the second conquest dynasty to rule the territory of China proper and roughly doubled the territory controlled by the Ming. The Manchus were formerly known as Jurchens, residing in the northeastern part of the Ming territory outside the Great Wall. They emerged as the major threat to the late Ming Dynasty after Nurhaci united all Jurchen tribes and declared the founding of the Qing Dynasty in 1636.

The Qing dynasty set up the Eight Banners system that provided the basic framework for the Qing military conquest. Li Zicheng's peasant rebellion captured Beijing in 1644, and the Chongzhen emperor, the last Ming emperor, committed suicide. The Manchus allied with a Ming general, Wu Sangui, to seize Beijing, which was made the capital of the Qing dynasty. They proceeded to subdue the Ming remnants in the south. The decades of Manchu conquest caused enormous loss of lives, and the economic scale of China shrank drastically. In total, the Qing conquest of the Ming (1618–1683) cost as many as 25 million lives.

The early Manchu emperors combined traditions of Central Asian rule with Confucian norms of traditional Chinese government and were considered a Chinese dynasty. The Manchus enforced a "queue order," forcing Han Chinese men to adopt the Manchu queue hairstyle. Officials were required to wear Manchu-style clothing, Changshan bannerman dress, and Tangzhuang, but ordinary Han civilians were allowed to wear traditional Han clothing. Bannermen could not undertake trade or manual labor; they had to petition to be removed from banner status. They were considered a form of nobility and were given annual pensions, land, and allotments of cloth.

The Kangxi emperor ordered the creation of the Kanxi Dictionary, the most complete dictionary of Chinese characters that had been compiled. Over the next half a century, all areas previously under the Ming Dynasty were consolidated under the Qing. Conquests in Central Asia in the eighteenth century extended territorial control. Between 1673 and 1681, the Kangxi emperor suppressed the revolt of the three feudatories, an uprising of three generals in Southern China who had been denied hereditary rule of large fiefdoms granted by the previous emperor. In 1683, the Qing staged an amphibious assault on southern Taiwan, bringing down the rebel kingdom of Tungning, which was founded by the Ming loyalist Koxinga (Zheng Chenggong) in 1662 after the fall of the Southern Ming, and had served as a base for continued Ming resistance in Southern China. The Qing defeated the Russians at Albanzin, resulting in the Treaty of Qing Empire.

By the end of the Qianlong emperor's long reign in 1796, the Qing Empire was at its zenith. The Qing ruled more than one-third of the world's population and had the largest economy in the world. By area, it was one of the largest empires ever. In the nineteenth century, the empire was internally restive, allowing the western treaty of China, under which Hong Kong was ceded to Britain and importation of opium (produced by British Empire territories) was allowed. Opium usage continued to grow in China, adversely affecting societal stability.

Subsequent military defeats and unequal treaties with other western powers continued even after the fall of the Qing Dynasty. Internally, the Taiping Rebellion (1851–1864), a quasi-Christian religious movement led by the "Heavenly King Hong Xiuquan," raided roughly a third of Chinese territory for more than a decade until they were finally crushed in the Third Battle of Nanking in 1864. This was one of the largest wars in the nineteenth century in terms of troop involvement; there was massive loss of life and a death toll of about twenty million. A string of civil disturbances followed, including the Punti-Hakka Clan wars, the Nian Rebellion, Dugan Revolt, and Panthay Rebellion. All rebellions were ultimately put down, but at enormous cost and with millions dead, seriously weakening the central imperial authority. The banner system that the Manchus had relied upon for so long failed. Banner forces were unable to raise new armies, but the Qing did raise new armies, which successfully crushed the challenges to Qing authority. China never rebuilt a strong central army, and many local officials became warlords who used military power to effectively rule independently in their provinces.

The next morning, Philip awoke overwhelmingly sad but hopeful that peace was to transpire at last. He had one last breakfast of egg and charcoaled ham wraps and coffee. He said goodbye to all the parents and gangs and proceeded to board a Dutch ship headed for Indochina.

King's Mountain

Cornwallis's defeat of Horatio Gates helped him decide to continue his campaign in the south and invade North Carolina. His army was screened to the right and the middle by Tarleton's British legion. Major Patrick Ferguson, probably Clinton's only confidant, was probably sent to keep an eye on Cornwallis, was well to the west of Cornwallis to cover the left flank. He had about 1,200 men. In the meantime, a Patriot force of 1,100 men headed by William Campbell headed east to confront Ferguson. They found him at Kings Mountain on October 7, 1780.

About a mile from their objective, they dismounted and approached the ridge in four separate columns. They proceeded undetected until they were about four hundred yards from Ferguson's position. Ferguson never had a chance. He led a bayonet charge, but they were mowed down by the Patriots. Ferguson tried to rally his men, but he quickly went down with eight bullet wounds that killed him. White flags went up, but avenging "Tarleton's no-quarter assault at Waxham," the Patriots also gave no quarter and proceeded to slaughter the British. Ferguson's losses were 157 dead and 163 badly wounded. The Patriots also captured 698 prisoners and 1,400 stands of arms. It was considered the turning point of the war in the South.

CARY

C ary decided she needed to get help. She needed help with her drinking and drug problems. She needed help with her relationship problems, which started with a sexual assault by her cousin when she was just thirteen. She decided to try a psychiatrist who was located in the Capitol Records building. She drove her roadster over from Brea and found parking on the street. She made her way up the elevator and was just in time for her appointment. On the way up the elevator, she had company. It was Early, who she despised, the Blind Samurai, a woman with a broken arm, a woman with a brace on her neck, a woman with a bandage on her head, a man with a broken leg, and a man in a wheelchair.

Her psychiatrist had experience treating those with PTSD from childhood trauma. They had their first session more than a week earlier, and she determined that Cary needed to work on her relationship problems and her childhood assault before they could deal with the alcohol and drugs. Starting with the assault, she had blocked much of it out of her memory.

Marty, the psychiatrist, decided to put Cary under hypnosis to see if she could recall the assault and deal with it directly in her conscious mind. "I'm counting down from one hundred. You are just thirteen. What is happening to you?"

"I am becoming sexually aware, and I seem to be attracted to girls, not boys. My cousin is about eighteen, and he is always hanging around our house. He's always following me to the bathroom or my bedroom. I hate him! One day I came in from swimming, and I'm in my bikini. He spots me from the street, and he comes up to our door. Before I can lock it, he forces his way in! He follows me to my bedroom and forces his way in.

"He warns me that I can't get away and that I better not scream—or he'd make me pay. He forces me on the bed and undoes his pants. He fondles my breasts and then forces his way inside of me. It happens so fast, and he is done in several minutes. I am screaming at this point, but he doesn't give a shit. He just gets up, pulls up his pants, and leaves."

Marty said, "At the count of ten, you will wake up and remember everything!" "That bastard—and the weird thing is he looks just like that bastard coworker of mine, Early!" She started to shriek louder and louder, and the whole building seemed to be shaking. At the front entrance, Cary saw a woman with a broken arm, a woman with a tourniquet on her neck, a woman with a bandage on her head, a man with a broken leg, and a man in a wheelchair. They were followed by the Blind Samurai. He was followed by none other than that bastard Early. The building continued to shake, and it suddenly seemed to list. *Oh my God! It is leaning! The Leaning Tower of Capitol Records!* Cary felt like she was walking on air. *Oh my God! The building is leaning. I didn't notice that when I went in. The Leaning Tower of Capitol Records!*

The next morning, Cary decided to take a trip to Pismo Beach, north of Santa Barbara. From Brea, the drive took about three hours. She checked into a hotel and had dinner. She ordered a dry martini, two chalupas, two tacos, and sides of beans and Spanish rice. She finished her meal and ordered another martini. After five drinks, she took a walk on the beach and smoked a joint. When she got back to her room, she snorted coke for several hours. She finally fell asleep.

The next morning, Cary went down to breakfast, ordered a Bloody Mary, and ate scrambled eggs, ham, hash browns, sourdough toast, and a latte. After breakfast, she went up to her room and snorted more coke. She put on her bikini, grabbed a towel, and went down to the beach. She found a lawn chair and ordered a dry gin martini.

The hotel was recommended by her psychiatrist and the psychiatric association, and the management and staff ignored the occasional abuse. Cary tripped the waiter as he went for her drink. He came back with her drink, and when he went to leave, she stabbed him in the butt with a fork.

Cary finished her drink, and Gaughy showed up. They decided to go up to her room and snort more coke. They went back to the beach and ordered drinks. This time, Gaughy had the honor of tripping the waiter. He brought their drinks back, and they both stabbed him in the butt with their forks.

They were having a good time and yukking it up, and then the dirty bastard Early showed up.

Cary slugged him in the gut and then the jaw, and he fell down on the beach. "Why'd you do that?"

"You look just like that bastard cousin of mine who raped me!"

"Oh, well, you feel better?"

"Yes, I feel great!"

"Well, that's good!"

The fat waiter showed up for more orders.

Gaughy slugged him in the gut and the jaw, and he went flying back and landed next to Early.

"Don't ask!" Early said.

COWPENS

After the disaster at Camden, Washington finally got to put his own man in place in the south: Nathanael Greene. Horatio Gates, an adjunct general, was in charge of supplies. He did, however, highly recommended that Daniel Morgan be brought back into action and promoted.

Morgan and Benedict Arnold were treated rather shabbily by Congress and were passed over for promotions in favor of foreigners. Washington and Greene both wholeheartedly supported the idea of bringing Morgan back and promoting him to general. Greene's strategy was to divide his forces and send Morgan west and south. He was supposed to go to Ninety Six, South Carolina, but when he heard that Tarleton would oppose him, he chose Cowpens, which was south of the Broad River.

Morgan had a force of about 1,100 men, and Tarleton had a similar force of 1,200. Morgan implemented a never-before-tried idea of placing his militiamen in front of the more disciplined Continentals. He also made it impossible for them to run far since the Broad River was unfordable. The night before the battle, Morgan went from campfire to campfire, asking the men to give him "three good shots, boys" and then fall back. Tarleton was still eight miles away, and they began their march shortly after midnight. They reached Cowpens at daybreak. Deploying for an early attack, he sent some dragoons forward to probe. Alert Patriot militia spotted them and promptly emptied fifteen saddles. The battle was on.

The British infantry moved in for the assault. When they came within fifty yards, the militia fired and fired again until the smoke cleared. When the British bayonets came forward, the first line of militia retreated in order back along the left flank. As the British moved forward, the second line held on for three volleys.

As Tarleton saw the first two lines running to the rear, he ordered the Seventeenth Light Dragoons to give chase. They were then met by Washington's cavalry; they turned the British mounts who went to the rear. Tarleton's front line was momentarily halted by the Continentals threw the Highlanders at the Patriots' right flank that was Howard's men. As this was going on, Morgan and Pickens rushed to the rear to shore up and bring forward the fleeing militias.

As the Highlanders charged, they were met with a bayonet charge from Howard's men. Pickens's militia came around the slope on the right flank to envelop the Highlanders. Washington's dragoons rejoined the battle on the Patriot left, actually coming up from the British right flank after having given Seventeenth Dragoons chase. They attacked Tarleton's light infantry and legion. Tarleton's entire infantry was retreating. He called in the dragoons again, but after they saw the soldiers fleeing, they galloped away. Tarleton put himself into action and had a kind of cut-and-slash battle with Washington, and then he fled the battle for good.

In a two-hour period, the British lost 110 killed and 229 wounded. They also lost more than eight hundred as prisoners. Morgan only lost twelve killed and sixty-one wounded. He promptly bagged Tarleton's entire baggage train, one hundred horses, and eight hundred muskets. Cornwallis was left without a cavalry unit. It was the first battle that involved a double envelopment since Hannibal's victory over the Romans in 216 BC.

General Morgan said, "We gave them a devil of a whipping."

Drapey's Vacation

D rapey decided to take his vacation by visiting his old friend Mike Hammer in Seattle. He took the tube train from his home in Santa Maria, California, and headed to Seattle. He arrived in Seattle and went straight to Mike's condo in downtown Seattle.

"Hey, Drapes, come on in. Can I get you a drink?"

"Hey, thanks, Mike. Yeah, I'll have a Seattle's Best coffee if you have any." "Sure, I'll just put on a pot. I have a young woman coming into the office. Want to tag along?"

"Sounds interesting. Sure, I'd love to."

At the office, they settled in and waited for the potential client.

A beautiful young woman walked in and said, "Is this the Hammer Investigation Firm?" "Sure is. Have a seat. This is my colleague Drapey Curtis."

"Has anyone told you that you look just like Dan Duryea?"

"Oh, a throwback?"

"Well, I have a collection of film noir on my film ring. Has anyone told you that you look just like Lauren Bacall?"

"Yes, she's one of my favorites. And, Mike, you look just like Humphrey Bogart. Well, now that that's established, what can I do for you, doll?"

"It's my sister. You see, she's come up missing. I was just at her place, and her keys and purse are on the counter, and her car is in the carport, but no Regina."

"You sure she didn't just go for a walk?"

"Yes, that's not like her at all."

"Well, my fees are five thousand a day plus expenses."

"Okay, my father will pay. He's with Powell, Lorre, and Greenstreet."

"Okay, well, let's go have a look. By the way, how do we get ahold of you?" "Just give me a whistle into your ring. You know how to whistle, don't you, Mike? Just put your lips together and blow."

They got into Mike's EMV and headed toward the Space Needle District. When they arrived at Regina's condo, her keys and purse were on the kitchen counter and her car was in the carport.

"Well, let's have a look around." Mike went into the first bedroom and found a dead body with a bullet between its eyes. "Ah, come into the bedroom, won't you, doll? Recognize him?" "Yeah, that's Regina's boyfriend, John Garland."

"You mean *the* John Garland?"

"Yes, and he did look and sound just like him. Well, not anymore! Regina looks just like Teresa Wright—so there's that too. I sense a pattern here. Any idea who he had the pleasure of his company with?"

"Yes, I suspect it was Regina's former boyfriend, Richard Widmark. You guessed it—that Richard Widmark, a spitting image."

"Well, this is getting interesting, doll. Any idea where he might have gone?" "I suspect he probably took Regina to Daddy's firm to extort some money." "Better call him and let him know we're on our way."

The EMV rode above a magnetic track covered with plants and trees. They were headed to the Green Lake area, north of Seattle.

"Notice all the beautiful, trellised terrain architecture covered with arbor? There are also coastal elk, deer, coyote, beaver, muskrat, blue heroin, white egrets, ducks, geese, swans, hawks, and eagles."

Drapey said, "Wow! You're a regular walking encyclopedia Britannica, aren't you, doll? "It's just the two-dollar version. You're Drapes. It's the least I can do."

When they arrived at Powell, Lorre, and Greenstreet, they were greeted at the door by two of the partners. After introductions, Mr. Greenstreet had the honor of taking them to meet their third—albeit dead–partner.

"Mike, I'm beginning to sense a pattern here as well."

"No kidding. Right between the eyes, pun intended. That blaggard ex-boyfriend transferred all of our firm's funds to an offshore account."

"Any idea where they might have moseyed off to next?"

Mr. Powell said, "I suspect he took Regina to my ex-wife Myrna Loy's house. Yes, that Myrna Loy."

"Why am I not surprised? Okay, gang, let's get started."

Myrna Loy lived on Vashon Island, and they had to take the hydroplaning ferry from the Edmonds Port. The ferry sailed five yards above the sound. They headed to Vashon Island. When they arrived, they figured they were about twenty minutes behind Richard and Teresa. When they arrived at Myra's house, Mike (Humphrey Bogart) asked Dan Duryea to reconnoiter the back way in case Richard tried to exit stage left.

Mike and Kate (Bogart and Bacall) went to the front and found the door wide-open. Inside, Myrna Loy was duct-taped to a dining room chair. Teresa was also duct-taped and on Richard's shoulder. Exit stage left.

They headed out the back to Myrna's heliport for her Sikorsky gyrocopter. Just then, they heard a sound from above. It was Dan Duryea. A plant pot caught wind and came crashing down on Widmark's head, narrowly missing Teresa Wright. As Duryea arrived on the scene, Bogart and Bacall also arrived. As Duryea was explaining the physics of the plant pot with much hilarity ensuing, Teresa was squirming something awful. They untied her, and she got a nice punch on the top of Widmark's head just as he had regained consciousness.

"Mike, we better go attend to Momma."

They left Duryea to see to Widmark and proceeded back to Myrna's house. They untied Myrna, and Widmark came flying in— under the restraint of Duryea. His revenge fell short, however, and Myrna got the first shot off, breaking the bridge of the blaggard's nose. She also connected with both eyes, which swelled shortly after impact.

"Well, all's well that ends well."

"Happy families are all the same."

William Powell and Myrna Loy remarried much to the delight of their daughters. And much to the surprise of our reading audience, Bacall and Bogart married as well. Regina (Teresa Wright) was bisexual all along, and she found a girlfriend and settled in—at least until the man of her dreams comes along. Much to the chagrin of her girlfriend? Well, that's another story altogether, isn't it?

Powell minus Lorre and Greenstreet compensated Mike and Drapes generously well. Drapey stayed on in Seattle and took in some deep sea fishing, visited the Space Needle, and went to Pikes Place Market and had some of Seattle's Best coffee. He then took the tube train home and returned to work with the Daniel Morgan Holographic Historical Project.

EARLY WASHES HIS HANDS

O
ut of the starlit blue came a man in a wheelchair, a man with a broken leg, a woman with a tourniquet on her neck, a woman with a turban-like bandage on her head, and a woman with a broken arm. They ran past a table with old incandescent light bulbs on it. This was a product of the holographic gang watching a W. C. Fields movie *It's a Gift*.

Fields said, "Quick, open the door—the blind detective from the hotel across the street is coming, and he'll break the door window."

The assistant rode his bicycle through the door and closed it behind him.

The blind detective broke through the glass window. "Who closed that damn door again?"

Fields's exasperation quickly gave out, and he said to his assistant, "I hate you! I hate you!"

The blind house dick sat next to a table of light bulbs and started swinging his cane. "Who put this damn table here?"

Alarmed, Fields replied, "That table has light bulbs on it, Mr. Muckle, dear." Mr. Muckle started swinging his cane and exclaimed, "Who put those damn light bulbs there again?"

Fields, seemingly oblivious to the blind dick's exasperation, said, "Please, Mr. Muckle, sweetheart. Dear, don't swing at the light bulbs!"

Mr. Muckle, seemingly incensed again, took a wild swing at the table and scored a direct hit on the light bulbs.

The injured gang were followed by the Blind Samurai. He was followed by Don Quixote, "The Man from La Mancha," and then Early. The Blind Samurai quickly chopped on the table of light bulbs, and Don Quixote dismantled the rest of the light bulbs.

Finally, Daniel Morgan came out and shouted, "Get the hell out of here!" Early went for his ring finger.

"Don't even think about it, Early, or you'll get a devil of a whipping." He produced a huge fist.

Early quickly withdrew his fingers from his ring finger. He proceeded out of the holographic studio, down the hallway, and into the bathroom. He removed his ring finger and pushed the orange alexandrite LED.

General Morgan disappeared into the starlit blue.

Around the World and the Seven Seas

Philip reached Bangkok, Indochina, about three weeks after he left China. He checked into his hotel and found an interpreter. He went to the restaurant and ordered dinner. He ordered charcoal chicken and beef wraps with rice and a baked potato. He had a strawberry sorbet for dessert. He also had a Thai sweet tea on ice. He had a daiquiri and met a young woman at the bar. He invited her up to his room, and they retired for the evening. The next morning, Philip had eggs Benedict, scones, coffee, and a sweet roll. He strolled out to a park with his interpreter and met a nice young couple who reminded him of Weng and Chin. He befriended them, and they asked if he'd be willing to escort them and sail with them to Kota Bharu. He agreed to meet them on the docks in the morning.

The next morning, Philip and his interpreter met up with the couple, Khampeng and Suriya, at the dock. They proceeded south to Kota Bharu. On the way, Philip found out the Khampeng was a princess and that her father had refused to let her marry a commoner. So, the couple eloped with Philip as their chaperone. When they arrived in Kota Bharu, the young couple were married and proceeded to go on their honeymoon.

Philip and his interpreter checked into a hotel, and he ordered lamb, sticky rice, sweet potatoes, baked apple with cinnamon spice, and a key lime pie. After dinner, he went to the bar and had a daiquiri. After several drinks, he retired for the night.

The next morning, Philip and his interpreter boarded a ship back to Bangkok. On the way, they heard that another ship had run into a monsoon rain. The ship ran aground, and many people perished. A few swam ashore and reportedly were making their way to Kota Bharu. When Philip arrived back in Bangkok, he ran into a terrible surprise. The king thought Philip was responsible for his daughter's abduction and ordered him executed. He was sent to death row. The magistrate questioned Philip, and he said he was only a chaperone and only found out on the trip that Khampeng was a princess.

The king almost let him go, but he wanted to confirm the story from his daughter and then annul her marriage. He would have to have his second daughter, still a virgin, succeed him to the throne. He then received the awful news that his second daughter was on the ship that had run aground in the storm. The king was beside himself with grief. He then received another report that the princess had died in a shipwreck as well. Things looked very grim for Philip.

As it turned out, the king's second daughter had survived the shipwreck by swimming ashore and making her way to Kota Bharu with the other survivors. His second daughter ended up not being in the other shipwreck. Another royal family received the horrible news that their daughter had perished in that accident. When the princess arrived home safely, her father was so grateful to have his two daughters alive and well he allowed the princess to remain married to the commoner and made him a prince. He also let Philip out of prison. Philip was sent off in a flag-waving twenty-one gun salute with a large crowd of the king's subjects. He proceeded to sail to Ceylon on another Dutch ship.

Burma, Thailand, Cambodia, Laos, and Vietnam were controlled by France since 1787 and called Cochinchina. Early in the seventeenth century, Alexandre de Rhodes, a Jesuit missionary, kicked off relations between Vietnam and France. It was during this time that Vietnam pushed south and claimed the Mekong Delta. Pierre Pigneau de Behaine petitioned the French government as a Catholic priest in 1787 to organize French volunteers to aid Nguyen Anh to retake lands his family lost to Tay Son Pigneau. He died, but his troops continued to fight until 1802.

French troops landed in Vietnam in 1858, and by the mid-1880s, they had established a firm grip over the northern region. From 1885 to 1895, Phan Đình Phùng led a rebellion against France. Nationalist sentiments intensified in Vietnam, especially during and after World War I, but all the uprisings and tentative efforts failed to obtain sufficient concessions from the French.

Around the World and the Seven Seas

For dinner, Philip ordered pork curry rice, and a large salad with cilantro, spinach, tomatoes, mushrooms, and red, green, and yellow peppers. He also ordered curds and whey. He had coffee and baklava and retired to his room.

The next day, Philip found his way to a plantation that grew hemp for ropes and clothes. The owners of the plantation happened to have a beautiful daughter. They invited Philip to dinner. It was love at first site for Philip and Hasitha.

Philip was walking on air when he returned to his hotel. He had dinner and retired to his room. Most of the plantations were owned by British citizens, but Hasitha's father owned theirs.

Philip returned to the plantation the next day and asked Haditha to go for a walk. He presented her with a beautiful diamond ring mounted on a silver band and asked her to marry him. She was overwhelmed and shed tears of happiness and said yes.

Haditha's parents were ecstatic and warmly received the news. They agreed to marry in a fortnight. They got married in a Buddhist church. They went to a retreat her parents owned for their honeymoon.

Philip and Hasitha moved into a small mansion on her father's estate and set up housekeeping. Philip set about seeing how he could help the family business. He went into the business office and found they had plenty of know-how and produced double-entry books and business plans. He went into the field and found they had good crop rotation, good soil conservation with the tilling of crops for nitrogen fixing, and good water use and conservation. The choice of crops was good and economically sound.

So, he found no real use for his help or services. He felt like a kept man. He decided to take Hasitha on a trip to India to clear his head. They decided to go to Pondicherry, which was close by. They took a ship and got in touch with wealthy friends of Hasitha's father. The friends invited them to their plantations to inspect their operations. Philip learned a lot, but he also learned that he was of little use to his father-in-law's plantation or business operations.

The one thing that stuck out the most was how the plantation systems succeeded with the use of serf labor. The conditions of these serfs varied, depending on the whims of the masters. This was quite disturbing to Philip since he had recently fought in a revolution that was supposed to free people and give them opportunities and a chance to succeed. Most importantly, it would give people their freedom, Philip thought he should take his wife to America with him, but he realized she would be treated as less than a second-class citizen. They would be rebuffed by society and ridiculed. Clearly, America was not an option. He could live the good life in Sri Lanka, but he would always be troubled by the serfdom. He also disliked the idea of being a kept man. When they returned from their trip, he decided he could educate himself on farming in case he did return to America someday.

They lived together in marital bliss for more than a year. One day changed everything. Haditha contracted malaria and fell ill. Her death was a tragedy for her parents, and Philip was beside himself. He really did miss her and felt such loss. He became mired in depression and alcohol. It was time for Philip to move on, and he chose to head to Kenya.

The first Europeans to visit Ceylon in modern times were the Portuguese. Lourenço de Almeida arrived in 1505, finding the island divided into seven warring kingdoms and unable to fend off intruders. The Portuguese founded a fort at the port city of Colombo in 1517 and gradually extended their control over the coastal areas. In 1592, the Sinhalese moved their capital to the inland city of Kandya, a good location to prevent invasion. Intermittent warfare continued through the eighteenth century, and lowland Ceylon was forced to convert to Christianity while the coastal Moors were religiously persecuted and forced to retreat to the central highlands while some of them desired to leave the country. The Buddhist majority disliked Portuguese occupation and its influences and welcomed any power who might rescue them and defeat the Portuguese. In 1602, therefore, when the Dutch captain Joris van Spilbergen landed, the king of Kandya appealed to him for help.

Franco-Siamese War (1893)

T erritorial conflict in the Indochinese peninsula for the expansion of French Indochina led to the Franco-Siamese War of 1893. In 1893, the French authorities in Indochina used border disputes, followed by the Paknam naval incident, to provoke a crisis. French gunboats appeared at Bangkok and demanded the cession of Lao territories east of the Mekong River. King Chulalongkorn appealed to the British, but the British minister told the king to settle on whatever terms he could get—and he had no choice but to comply. Britain's only gesture was an agreement with France guaranteeing the integrity of the rest of Siam. In exchange, Siam had to give up its claim to the Thai-speaking Shan region of northeastern Burma to the British and cede Laos to France.

DUTCH PRESENCE

In 1669, the Dutch attacked in earnest, but it ended with an agreement (which was disrespected by both parties), and it was not until 1656 that Colombo fell. By 1660, the Dutch controlled the whole island except the kingdom of Kandya. The Dutch (who were Protestants) persecuted the Catholics (the leftover Portuguese settlers) but left the Buddhists, Hindus, and Muslims alone. However, they taxed the people far more heavily than the Portuguese had done. A mixed Dutch-Sri Lankan people known as Burgher peoples are the legacy of Dutch rule. In 1669, the British sea captain Robert Knox landed by chance on Ceylon and was captured by the king of Kandya. He escaped nineteen years later and wrote an account of his stay. This helped bring the island to the attention of the British.

British Rule

During the Napoleonic Wars, Great Britain, fearing that French control of the Netherlands might deliver Ceylon to the French, occupied the coastal areas of the island with little difficulty in 1796. In 1802, by the Treaty of Amiens the Dutch part of the island was ceded to Britain, and it became a Crown colony. In 1803, the British invaded the kingdom of Kandya in the First Kandyan War, but they were bloodily repulsed. In 1815, Kandya was occupied in the Second Kandyan War, ending Ceylonese independence.

Following the bloody suppression of the Uva Rebellion, the Kandyan peasantry were stripped of their lands by the Wastelands Ordinance, a modern enclosure movement, and reduced to penury. The British found that the uplands of Sri Lanka were very suited to coffee, tea, and rubber cultivation, and by the mid-nineteenth century, Ceylon tea had become a staple of the British market, bringing great wealth to a small class of white tea planters. To work the estates, the planters imported large numbers of Tamil workers as indentured laborers from south India, who soon made up 10 percent of the island's population. These workers had to work in slave-like conditions and live in line rooms, which were not very different from cattle sheds.

The British colonists favored the semi-European Burghers, certain high-caste Sinhalese, and the Tamils who were mainly concentrated to the north of the country, exacerbating divisions and enmities that have survived ever since. Nevertheless, the British also introduced democratic elements to Sri Lanka for the first time in its history. The Burghers were given some degree of self-government as early as 1833. It was not until 1909 that constitutional development began with a partly elected assembly—and not until 1920 that elected members outnumbered official appointees.

Universal suffrage was introduced in 1931—over the protests of the Sinhalese, Tamil and Burgher elite who objected to the common people being allowed to vote.

DRAPEY

D rapey decided to visit Santa Marie when he heard that the city rangers were harassing the homeless. He left Brea and headed north. When he reached Santa Maria, he went straight to the town center and parked in the parking lot.

The rangers were rousting a homeless man from a ramp between stairs. They IDed him and sent him out into the pouring rain. He soon found out that the city had decided to eliminate park benches by the library, parks, and city streets. If they found out someone was at the bus terminal without a ticket, they would send them out rain or shine.

The city budgeted for extra ranger hires and for overtime. They hired an extra accountant to keep track of the overtime. The city council busied themselves passing ordinances designed to eliminate the presence of the homeless. They also passed a mission statement that included a top priority of "low profiling" the homeless. The effect was to have the homeless consider the rangers as "pricks." The city and the rangers felt that they had an epidemic on their hands, and this particular group of homeless people was a virulent strain.

The virulent strain had wild green eyes and possessed the ability to levitate, space travel, and could easily transport telekinesis. Drapey joined the group as an observer and witnessed his first telekinesis demonstration. He saw a green-eyed homeless man possess several rangers. Like *Being John Malkovich,* he had them dancing to the Beer Barrel Polka:

Beer Barrel Polka (Roll Out the Barrel)

> Roll out the barrel, roll out the barrel of beer.
> Roll out the barrel, roll out the barrel of cheer.
> Roll out the barrel, roll out the barrel of rum.
> Roll out the barrel, roll out the barrel of fun.
> Roll out the barrel, and the gang's all here!

Drapey spent the night outdoors, had breakfast made from their organic garden, and headed home. *The Comic Opera of the City Rangers* continued to amuse him as he played the Beer Barrel Polka and the Stein Song on the way home. All in all, it was a fun vacation.

FAITH

Running Bear and his family helped the freed slaves make their way across Pennsylvania. Faith, who was now known as Little Black Bear, along with her family, helped in the escape. They all dressed as Indians. They separated with some in wagons, some on horses, and some on foot. Faith and her family were on an eighteen-day vacation from the plantation, and other slaves temporarily took their place.

As they returned, Faith was fishing for trout on a small stream. She somehow lost her balance with the fishing strand around her ankle. As she got back on her feet, a large trout took bait and yanked her into the stream. She ended up snagging the large trout. With Running Bear's catch and her family's catches, they ended up having a nice dinner.

Running Bear and his family returned to western Pennsylvania, and Faith and her family returned to the Stevens's plantation. Mr. Stevens really missed Faith and needed her good advice on plantation matters.

Faith recommended that Mr. Stevens sell the plantation and free the slaves. She also recommended buying a customhouse, warehouses, and docks up in Baltimore. She recommended accepting Continental currency along with British pounds. She predicted the States would win the war—and the French would bail out the Continental currency with gold and silver even though they had a problem with fiat money themselves. It turned out exactly as Faith predicted, and Mr. Stevens ended up with his full share of revenue. When Hamilton started buying up all the other bankrupt customhouses, Stevens was able to hold on to his and profit greatly from it.

Faith helped her family and the Stevens family move to Baltimore. Faith was correct about freeing the slaves, and it saved room and board on Mr. Stevens's dime. The slaves rented at first, but almost all of them eventually bought houses. Since they no longer had crops and livestock, they had to buy all their own food. They supplemented this by growing gardens and fishing in the bay. She took over the accounting and bookkeeping, doing double-entry books that no one else could understand. It saved them money, and they were more profitable than their neighbors. The former slaves were all hired by the new company, including Faith, the accountant, and her family.

Faith, Running Bear, and Little Black Bear decided to visit Running Bear's uncle Great Bear and the tribe. They loaded up the duty-free wagons and proceeded along the road blazed by Colonel Morgan, the wagon master. They had gone about eighty miles before reaching the Kentucky border. They decided to go skinny-dipping in a cool spring that had a warm swimming hole.

They proceeded along the Cumberland Trail and reached the Cumberland Gap. They got there just in time since the tribe was suffering from an epidemic. Faith was able to supply her medicinal remedy and thus became the first honorable medicine woman. They also had a supply of soda water, quinine, and the epidemic was soon in remission. There were a lot of grateful people.

They unloaded the wagon, which had a lot of corn and wheat meal for bread, chicken, beef, tobacco, marijuana, peyote, rum, whiskey, port wine, and beer. Their dance ceremony included peyote to levitate and time travel in hallucinogenic bliss. Faith was able to entertain them with their astrological signs pointed out in the night sky, and she read their tea leaves for their monthly astrological horoscope.

They danced their peace dance and filled their pipes with tobacco and marijuana to relax and conjure up the Great Spirit. This was in gratitude for all of their great fortune. One of the tribesmen was thrown from his horse when it got spooked by a rattlesnake. He broke his leg in the fall. Faith was able to set his leg with a cast made of gypsum from the entrance of a nearby cave just as Dr. Germaine had shown her in the Harlem Hills.

The vacation went well, and Little Black Bear, Running Bear, and Great Red Bear proceeded along the Cumberland Trail and found their favorite swimming hole. Running Bear and Little Black Bear stopped to skinny-dip, and Great Red Bear continued ahead on the Cumberland Trail. After swimming and relaxing by the stream, Little Black Bear and Running Bear swore allegiance for better or worse until death do they part. They sealed their romantic love as being forever and ever. They now had a secret engagement. They rejoined their uncle and proceeded on to Baltimore.

Little Black Bear, Running Bear, and Great Red Bear joined Faith's family in prayer and meditation and celebrated with a hearty meal and lots to drink. Running Bear and Great Red Bear loaded their duty-free wagon and proceeded to Pennsylvania to supply Running Bear's family with provisions. As was fitting, Running Bear ran alongside his uncle. Faith returned to her accounting and payroll work for Mr. Stevens. Let the good times roll!

Around the World and the Seven Seas

Philip caught a Dutch ship to Kenya and landed at Mombasa. He checked into a hotel and found an interpreter. He then crossed Anatolia and Persia and went on to India, Indonesia, and Malaysia.

Portuguese colonization began in 1505 when Dom Francisco de Almeida captured Kilwa, an island south of Tanzania. The Portuguese presence served as the conduit to the Asia spice trade and allowed them to have a strategic advantage to disrupt transport of enemy shipping or demand heavy tariffs that kept their market advantage.

In 1593, Fort Jesus was constructed in Mombasa. This fort was captured by Arabs in 1698, but it was recaptured by the Portuguese in 1728. The Omanis eventually expelled the Portuguese for good. By the time Philip traveled the world, the Spanish and the Portuguese were weakening and losing the world colonization race. He had a dinner of steak, potatoes, and a large spinach salad with cilantro, tomatoes, hot peppers, mushrooms, onions, and a vinaigrette dressing. He had a deep, rich Kenyan coffee and a lemon custard pie and retired for the night.

The next day, needing a little adventure in his life, he set off for a safari of big game hunting. Kenya was colonized by the Dutch and the Arabs. Philip was with the Dutch, and the safari help and guides were Kenyan serfs. Philip did not want to shoot elephants or giraffes. He was, however, interested in rhinos or water buffalo. They traveled in a caravan with wagons, steers, and horses. At night, they listened to the howling and laughter of hyenas.

With their morning coffee, Philip and his guides planned their strategy for finding the game and setting up for the shoot. They set out on horses, wary of elephants and other big game. They followed a river and then set out on a ridge. They found a low valley with trees and bushes and proceeded to wait for some big game. Just as they were about to give up, as the sun was going down, a water buffalo trotted into range. Philip mounted his gun on a tripod and got off a shot. The first, and only, shot hit the target, piercing its heart. They dressed the buffalo and put the meat in their wagons. They were back at their lodge by nine thirty and had an excellent water buffalo meal with salad, potatoes, and beer.

Kenyan civilization was quite advanced even before foreigners came and traded or colonized. Their productive capabilities in ironworking, agriculture, hunting, and fishing were enough to support early city-states in the whole region. This included the Cushitic ironworkers and the food cultures of Mombasa, Malindi, and Zanzibar. This inevitably led to trade with the Arab states that were more seaworthy. After the trade began with Arab and Persian traders, a more culturally divergent society emerged as the Bantu culture.

Swahili is a Bantu language with some Arab and Persian words mixed in. The Swahili culture developed in the cities and towns, which included Pate, Malinda, Mombasa, and later Zanzibar. Wealth flowed into the region as the merchant cities became intermediaries for Arab, Persian, Indian, Indonesian, Malaysian, African, Chinese, and Japanese merchants who enhanced the culture and increased the wealth in the region.

Although Kenya was a fairly advanced civilization, its location and the advent of the spice trade eventually led to colonization. The Portuguese first explored the area in 1498 when Vasco da Gama visited Mombasa. The voyage also reached India on that same trip. The spice routes to Asia were originally controlled by the Venetians and the republic of Venice. They used the Persian Gulf and the Red Sea and then land routes to the Mediterranean Sea. The other land route was controlled by the Ottoman Turks. By 1780, Kenya was somewhat independent, but it still had a lot of foreign influence. The Arabs probably had the most influence. Of the European colonialists, the power had shifted from the Portuguese to the Dutch. The Dutch probably prevailed until the English dominated late in the nineteenth century. The shifting of power in Europe at this juncture saw the Spanish and Portuguese in their zenith, but their power started to wane slowly over the next century. Their power and influence were being replaced by the Dutch, the English, and the French. Of the three, the English were the most prolific in creating the British Empire.

The Swahili Bantus had developed a modern culture and civilization based on natural resources and the Swahili city-state culture that became productive with these resources. This inevitably led to trade and commerce, which eventually led to foreign influence and eventual colonization.

After a satisfying, albeit short, visit, Philip departed Nairobi, Kenya, on an Arab ship. They were headed up the Red Sea for departure to Suez (El Suweis). They landed and procured their traveling companions, namely, camels. The camel is an ornery beast, but the Arabs told Philip to smoke their hashish and blow it in the camel's nose to keep it calm. The single-hump camels carried the luggage, and the double-humped camels bore the riders. Philip's camel was hard to figure which way was his fore and which way his aft. He boarded the camel and found he was faced the wrong way. The camel rose up and proceeded to head in the opposite way of the caravan.

Philip faced the caravan, but due to the substance, he thought they were headed to the back of the caravan.

When Philip finally found his bearing, he turned the ornery beast around and headed to the left of the caravan. He finally got it to go left and ended up at the head of the caravan. This, of course, wouldn't do if they could end up almost anywhere but Port Said. After they convinced Philip's camel to move to the rear, they were on their way again. Beautiful songs and trumpets heralded their travel with Islamic sounds. Sunset was near, and they stopped to camp for the night. After more hashish and some arak alcohol, Philip fell sound asleep.

For breakfast, they had hummus and falafel with figs, dates, olives, chickpeas, and grapes. They mounted the camels and headed for Port Said.

EYALET OF EGYPT

A fter the great empires of Egypt had waned and the first the Greeks and then the Romans conquered the area, Egypt was susceptible to foreign conquest and rule. The local customs, religion, culture, and agriculture allowed Egypt to maintain a fairly high level of independence. The Eyalet of Egypt came as a result of the Ottoman conquest of Mamluk, Egypt. In 1516–1517 the Ottoman-Mamluk war resulted in the conquest of Egypt, and during the same period, the Ottomans also conquered Syria.

In 1780, Egypt was part of the Ottoman Empire, but they lived fairly independently and governed locally. Because of the strength of the Mamluk military caste system, Egypt was very difficult for the Ottomans to control. Egypt remained a self-governed state within the empire. Egypt remained in this semiautonomous state from 1517 until 1867—with the exception of French Napoleonic rule from 1789 to 1805.

Russia

Philip then boarded a Russian ship headed up the Mediterranean, the Black Sea, and Yalta, Ukraine. When he arrived, he checked into a hotel and found an interpreter. He then went to dinner and ordered pelmeni, piroshki, borscht, and a baked potato. He went to the bar and ordered vodka with a beer chaser. After several rounds of drinks, he retired for the night.

The next morning, his interpreter had an idea. Instead of staying at a hotel, they could go to a B&B to save money. They strolled into Yalta and found a nice family-owned place that was run by a serf family. As they checked out the place, Philip noticed that the maid was quite beautiful and a hard worker. She seemed to have an eye on him, but he thought it was just concern for customer satisfaction.

The girl and her parents were serfs owned by the owner's family. That family owned a large number of B&Bs and made their living that way. Philip and his interpreter decided it was a nice place to stay. They sat down to lunch and had beef Stroganoff, Olivier salad, and Medovik honey cake and coffee for dessert.

Philip's new interest was named Nadia. He asked how they could win their freedom. She told him they were like indentured servants, and the only way to win their freedom was to be bought out. Philip considered the cost of the three people and decided to buy their freedom. Philip and his interpreter sat down for dinner and then retired for the night.

For breakfast, Philip had eggs Benedict, ham, potatoes, blini with raspberry compote, and coffee. After breakfast asked Nadia if they could summon the owners. Her parents sent her to fetch them. Philip and the B&B owners came to terms, and he bought the family intact. It was easy for the B&B owners to replace that family with another indentured servant contract that would cost nothing. They thought they really had something over on Philip since he didn't understand their country. Philip's true intention, however, was ask for Nadia's hand in marriage.

Philip asked Nadia's parents, Olga and Vladimer, if he could ask for their daughter's hand in marriage. They were very pleased and gave him their permission. He asked Nadia to go for a walk, and at a park bench, he showed her a diamond ring mounted on a band of silver and asked for her hand in marriage. Nadia was happily surprised and had tears of joy, and she agreed to marry Philip. They decided to get married in Monte Carlo and move to America with her parents.

RUSSIAN EMPIRE

B y 1780, Russia was a first-rate world power. Catherine the Great was in power and was continuing the Russian modernization started by Peter the Great. She was greatly influenced by the French Enlightenment and continued Peter's empire expansion.

Peter ruled from 1672 to 1725, and he brought European autocracy by forming a nine-member senate with the primary goal of raising taxes. The nine senators were each given a province to raise the revenue, and the plan was very successful. His first conquest was against the Ottoman Turks. He captured Kiev and built a great navy on the Black Sea.

Russia stretched all the way from the Baltic Sea to the Pacific Ocean. Peter was also able to pacify the Siberian Tribes. He formed a secret alliance with the Polish-Lithuanian commonwealth and Denmark. In 1703, he started to build the great city of St. Petersburg as Russia's new capital. He attacked Sweden, and they sued for peace in 1721. Peter named himself czar and officially became emperor of Russia.

During his final years as emperor, Peter set about reforming the government by promulgating the table of ranks, creating *"administrative Collegia"* (ministries), and subduing the power of the Greek Orthodox Church. He also helped consolidate his empire by attacking the declining Persian Safavid Empire in what became known as the Russo-Persian war. Peter was able to wrest control of much of the Caucasus and Caspian Sea region. Twelve years later, all this had been ceded back to the Persian Empire.

Peter brought in many of Western Europe's top scientists, philosophers, and engineers, but this eventually led to Western resentment that culminated in expulsion of foreigners after the Napoleonic Wars a century after Peter's rule. Peter managed to greatly increase tax revenue, but building his empire cost even more. His revenue went from nine million rubles in 1724 to forty million by 1794, but his expenses were at forty-nine million. They ended up borrowing from Amsterdam. Peter was succeeded by his second wife, Catherine, and she ruled from 1725 to 1727. She was followed by Peter II, a minor grandson, ruling from 1727 to 1730, and then Anna, the daughter of Ivan V, ruled from 1730 until 1740.

Finally, in 1741, Russia was to once again have a great leader. Catherine the Great was the German wife of the German prince who inherited the throne, but he was simpleminded, and Catherine had him executed and assumed power. She began by continuing Peter's enlightenment involvement patronizing the arts, science, and learning. She expanded the Russian nobility by promulgating the Charter of Gentry. She also further reduced the power of the Greek Orthodox Church and put what remained on a tight budget.

Catherine continued Peter's policy regarding Poland and Lithuania, extending Russia's support of the Targowica Confederation. This led to a "peasants' revolt" inspired by a Cossack named Pugachev with the cry of "Hang the landlords!" Catherine subsequently crushed the revolt. Catherine spent heavily on her foreign intrusions, and like the other "enlightened" European despots, she extended her power and control. She also subdued the Baltic States for access to the sea. She extended the fight Peter started in wresting control of the Baltic and waged war against Persia, invading Georgia and controlling the Baltic territories.

Philip, his fiancé, and her parents boarded a Greek ship and set sail for Monte Carlo. When they arrived in Monte Carlo, Philip received the news that America had won its freedom and was now the United States of America. It was two years late, but the news was greatly received anyway.

Philip and Nadia got married in a Greek Orthodox Church and honeymooned right there in Monte Carlo. For their wedding feast, they had chicken Basquaise, honey-glazed pork roast with apples, a lentil salad with pork, Cheaujolais chorizo bread, and for their wedding cake they had piece *Montee Croquembouche*, a tower of cream puffs with spun sugar and vanilla creme. Vladimer proposed a toast to the new couple with Mumm, a dry white champagne.

They went by carriage across France, stopping off in Paris, and they finally arrived in Bordeaux, boarded a French ship, and set sail for New York.

Europe

In 1780, King Louis XVI was popular and in full control in France. His wife, however, was of German descent and from Austria, which was often in a state of war with France. So, Marie Antoinette was not popular like her husband. This may be part of the reason that Louis also declined in popularity. The main reason that Louis lost his popularity was due to fiat money. It sharply devalued the value of the franc, and the money devaluations led to widespread poverty that ended with Marie Antionette exclaiming, "Let them eat cake."

In 1780 France was fairly stable and benefitted from its participation in the American Revolutionary War. They regained control of several Caribbean Islands after the peace treaty with Britain.

Germany was separated into many principalities, which were known as the Holy Roman Empire of Germany. Several of the kings sold mercenaries to the British during the Revolutionary War. It ultimately led to the Prussian Empire. In 1772, Prussia took control of the eastern territories of the Polish-Lithuanian province, sharing the partition with Catherine the Great of Russia.

Spain was at a zenith of its power by 1780, colonizing Cuba, Florida, Mexico, Venezuela, Columbia, Peru, Bolivia, Chile, Argentina, and the Philippines.

During the eighteenth century, the power, wealth, and influence of the Netherlands declined. A series of wars with the more powerful British and French neighbors weakened it. The UK seized the North American colony of New Amsterdam and renamed it "New York." There was growing unrest and conflict between the Orangists and the Patriots. The French Revolution spilled over after 1789, and a pro-French Batavian Republic was established in 1795–1806. Napoleon made it a satellite state, the kingdom of Holland (1806–1810), and later simply a French imperial province.

The English won the seven-year French and Indian war. They won Canada and negotiated for some of the Caribbean. The British lost their American colonies, and they did not win the Revolutionary War. However, they continued to trade manufactured goods for raw materials with the American colonies.

During, and shortly after, the American Revolutionary, War the British grew in power due to the industrial revolution. England of the 1780s was in some respects "modern," an "age of machinery" as Carlyle maintained. It was an England of rapid industrial change where a growing population was being drawn to the expanding towns and cities of the north and midlands. It was a land of canals and newly surfaced roads that fed economic growth. But it was also an "old" country in which going to a different part of the country was viewed as going to a foreign land and where a belief in the supernatural remained.

In the 1780s, the tensions between change and continuity were unresolved, and in some ways, they remained unresolved in 1846. These pressures were more obvious outside of England. In Scotland, Wales, and Ireland, the distinction between innovation and tradition was starker, and resistance to change often took on a strongly nationalist character. Attitudes to particular crops grown in Ireland illustrate this distinction. The cultivation of turnips was seen as innovative by many rural laborers and, perhaps more importantly, as an English innovation. Turnips were destroyed in the fields just as some believed they were destroying their lives. By contrast, the potato, introduced by the English in the seventeenth century, had become an accepted and essential part of Irish cultural and dietary life. It is not surprising that some nationalists of the Young Ireland movement were able to represent the potato famines of the 1840s as part of a deliberate policy of genocide by English government. For many contemporaries, Britain was a country of opposing poles: improvement and resistance, modernity and tradition, change and continuity, Englishness and cultural and linguistic nationalism, north and south, and rich and poor. As is always the case, reality was far less clear-cut and far more complex than the rhetoric suggested.

In June 1780, the most destructive urban riots in English history erupted onto the streets of London. Sparked by resistance to the Catholic Relief Act of 1778, the riots soon escalated into a sustained assault on government properties and institutions. Fueled by popular resentment against the war with America, the mob set fire to the private houses of members of Parliament, central London prisons, and the tollbooths on bridges. At one stage, even the Bank of England was attacked. For several nights, it seemed as if the whole of London was ablaze; the country was on the verge of revolution. In the words of one newspaper, "Everything served to impress the mind with ideas of universal anarchy and approaching desolation." Professor Ian Haywood argued that this spectacle of apocalyptic destruction gave the Gordon riots their cultural power and mystique, evoking memories of the Great Fire of 1666 and anticipating both the French Revolution and the Bristol Reform-Bill riots of 1831.

Guilford Courthouse

organ's troops and the British prisoners and captured
supplies and horses retreated from Cowpens through
rainy weather. They rejoined Greene at Guilford
Courthouse. Morgan was suffering from severe sciatica, and he
could no longer walk. Greene ordered him back to his Virginia farm.
Morgan appraised Greene of his Cowpens strategy and retired from
the war effort. Greene, having a limited number of troops, retreated
back to the Dan River and ordered all boats procured and crossed the
Dan in good order. As Cornwallis approached the Dan River, he saw
that all the boats had crossed the river. He withdrew to Hillsboro and
detached some of his troops to secure communications and supply
lines back to Camden and Charleston.

With reinforcements, Greene decided he could again risk battle
and returned to Guilford Courthouse. He now had about 4,300 men.
Greene drew up his battle plan as advised by Morgan. He had three
lines of defense. He placed his immediate charges on the third line.
Before the British arrived, Greene did as Morgan did and strolled
along his front line of North Carolina militiamen, admonishing them
to give "three rounds, my boys, and then you may fall back."

Cornwallis advanced early in the morning with Lee's Legion of the Americans falling back before them. As Lee pulled back, Cornwallis's men approached the front line of North Carolina militiamen. The Americans opened up with two cannons, and the British responded in kind; the battle had commenced. As British and Hessian troops advanced, the American militia responded with two volleys. The British responded with one of their own. The British then brandished bayonets, and the front lines retreated.

The British advanced, but they began to receive fire and soon realized they were receiving fire from both their right and left flanks from Virginia militiamen. The Virginia militiamen, Kirkwood light militiamen, and Washington's cavalry all retreated in good order, taking prearranged positions on their right flank; they were then driven well to the northeast, isolated from the rest of the Patriot forces.

The British left flank smashed into the second line of Stevens's brigade, and the Americans fled. Leslie was held up as he dealt with this resistant second line. Webster advanced toward the third line. The British and Hessians were confronted with the Virginia third line and were driven back. Greene's Morgan-inspired battle plan had gone off without a hitch.

The Virginians of Lawson's brigade were finally overwhelmed by Leslie and supported by the rear reserve brigade of O'Hara. The American left was overwhelmed by Webster. A wounded O'Hara caused his replacement, Lieutenant Colonel Duncan Stuart, to take command of the British center line. As a gap developed in the American center line, Stuart led a charge toward the courthouse. The American line seemed overwhelmed but Colonel Washington's cavalry counterattacked. Stuart was killed, and the wounded O'Hara took over. Colonel Howard of Cowpens fame attacked O'Hara's shattered regiments and was saved by Leslie. Cornwallis ordered an artillery grapeshot attack over the objections of O'Hara. He knew some of his troops would be killed or wounded, but he felt his troops would stand. He was right, and the Americans fell back to regroup.

Cornwallis ordered on final attack, and Greene ordered a withdrawal. The Virginia Continentals fired as they withdrew. The battle was pretty much over, but Webster was fatally wounded.

Cornwallis lost about 25 percent of his army, which was a devastating blow! Greene's tactic of preserving his army had worked. The British lost ninety-three dead and 493 wounded. The Americans lost seventy-eight dead and 183 wounded. Cornwallis had driven Greene off the battlefield—but at a great cost. Greene regrouped and led his army south toward South Carolina. Cornwallis was pretty much done with the Carolinas and marched to the coast, intending to take the battle to Virginia.

Early

arly decided to take his vacation at an Indian gambling casino
in Chamush, next to Lake Cachuma near Santa Barbara. He
was going to a private resort to play straight-hand five-card
poker. He started playing and soon noticed that he would lose every
good hand he played! Then he noticed the tiny camera lens on the
wall behind him! It also had a wallflower just below it that gave either
a thumbs-up or thumbs-down. Early switched his chair around the
table and began to win every hand he played.

The other players began to lose every hand they played! They
were, however, private club hacks playing the fraud! After several
hands and a chip bonanza, Early decided to cash his chips in early. He
strolled out into the dark parking lot and checked if there was anyone
following him. He was virtually surrounded. He quickly jumped into
his electromagnetic vehicle and started toward the exit.

The Private Club Hack was coming straight for him. Early quickly
evaded an accident along with a woman with a broken arm, a woman
with a tourniquet around her neck, a woman with a bandage on her
head, a man with a broken leg, and a man in a wheelchair. They
were followed by the Blind Samurai. The Private Club Hack missed
Early and the gang and ran into a guardrail. Early rushed up to the

vehicle, opened the door, gave a quick uppercut to the hack's right eye and a series of rabbit punches to his ribs. He told the hack to tell the authorities that he sustained his injuries in the car crash—or he'd regret it once he went to prison!

The city rangers came to the rescue and read the hack his rights. They congratulated the injured gang, the Blind Samurai, and Early and gave them all tickets to the Ranger's Ball. Early asked if there was a place to wash his hands. Early spent the rest of his vacation in Pismo Beach and Avila Beach with Gaughy and Cary.

Washington's Camp Followers

The Butcher, the Baker, the Candlestick Maker, the Fabric and Dress Maker, the Blacksmith, the Wagon Maker, and the Stable Livestock Caregiver were all part of Washington's Camp Followers. His winter quarters were in Pequannock, south of Pompton Plains. Colonel van Cortlandt made his headquarters in the Yellow Tavern. The first winter quarters was in Morristown, the second was Valley Forge, the third was Morristown and then Pequannock. Unlike the previous winter quarters, Pequannock was easily attended by the Camp Followers. The most important group of the Camp Followers were the "women of the night." Washington's troops and officers were frequent visitors to the brothels. One night, one of the women went missing. She was found dead near the Yellow Tavern. At first, the officers were suspected. Washington called Detective Inspector Summers to come down from Morristown and see if he could catch the culprit.

Detective Summers quickly realized that no officers were involved. He concentrated his investigative skills on the Camp Followers. He used a process of elimination so he could home in on the suspect. The Butcher was a frequent visitor to the brothel in exchange for his meat and was seemingly a satisfied customer. The Baker supplied

the women with breakfast, and since he didn't charge them, his wife
suspected that he too was taking advantage of their services. Despite
his claims to the contrary, his wife was sure of it and incensed and
livid! The Candlestick Maker provided lighting for the bordellos, but
he abstained from the services due to his religious convictions. He
had been quite fond of one of the ladies and was heartbroken when
she seemingly disappeared. The Blacksmith was a frequent visitor
and always paid handsomely for their services. The Dressmaker made
clothes and uniforms for the troops as well as beautiful clothes and
silk nighties and underthings for the girls. The Dressmaker was a
good seamstress and provider of nice clothing for the girls. The Forge
Worker also frequented the ladies and paid well for their services. The
Wagon Maker was a fanatic religious worshiper, and he didn't pay any
visits—or at least it was assumed so.

The livestock woman, aside from her duties of milking, egg
gathering, chicken and beef provider to the butcher, served also as a
madam to the ladies. By a process of elimination, Detective Summers
ruled out the Butcher and the Baker—but not his wife. The Candlestick
Maker remained on the list due to the disappearance of the lovely lady,
the Dressmaker could have had some jealousy, the Wagon Maker was
a weak suspect, and the Stable Woman and madam were also weak
suspects.

On the night in question, it ended up the Baker's wife was with
both him and the Butcher. The Stable Woman ended up having gone
to Morristown to sell some eggs and meat so she too was eliminated.
That left just the Candlestick Maker and the Wagon Maker. Fearful
that he was suspected, the Candlestick maker decided to make a
move. He put a few things in the toolbox of the wagon—all the
time being watched by Detective Summer. Summer thought he was
making a break for it. He decided he couldn't lose one of his last
two suspects. Instead of leaving the camp, he headed straight for
the brothel. Detective Summer thought he was either visiting a lady,
which would have eliminated him as a suspect, or was possibly up to

no good! As the Candlestick Maker hitched up in front of the lady's bordello, he started rummaging through his toolbox. Highly alarmed, the inspector snuck up to the wagon, and the hair raised on the back of his neck when he saw the Candlestick Maker make his way into the bordello. In the nick of time, he was able to thwart the devil—who was about to put a knife in one of the girls—and promptly place him under arrest.

Washington, of course, was very pleased with the result and directed a few of his men to accompany the inspector and his prisoner back to Morristown. The Candlestick Maker was imprisoned and immediately scheduled for trial. In a plea agreement for life without parole and hard labor, he confessed to the murders of a total of thirteen women, including his love fancy. His plea agreement also stipulated that he must provide the gravesites of all the women—or it would be nullified. He provided a map, and they did find all of the bodies to return to friends or relatives. He would have been considered America's first serial killer, but no one actually knew his name!

YORKTOWN

The Patriots' cause in Virginia was not going well. Benedict Arnold was pretty much having his way rampaging through the eastern and central regions of the state. Cornwallis was also marching northward from Wilmington, North Carolina. Starting in May, Washington ordered Major General Lafayette to Virginia with General Anthony Wayne and 2,200 troops. Cornwallis joined Arnold at Petersburg, and the British troops in Virginia numbered more than seven thousand. Lafayette managed to avoid any major provocation with the much larger British force.

Cornwallis's move to Yorktown was immediately reported to Washington by Lafayette. Washington could immediately see the strategic value of isolating Cornwallis at Yorktown. Washington received a letter from Admiral Francois de Grasse in the West Indies. He would sail to Virginia and stay there until October 15. Washington created a diversion against Clinton by moving American and French troops south to Staten Island. Leaving a few troops behind to continue the diversion, American and French troops marched south through New Jersey, headed for Baltimore and then Yorktown.

Clinton learned of the deception on September 5, but by then, it was too late to catch them. Washington learned that de Grasse and three thousand troops had arrived in Chesapeake Bay, but Washington still worried the de Barres sailing out of Rhode Island might be intercepted by Graves sailing from New York. Instead of throwing his entire fleet against the French, Graves chose to follow the English predilection to form the "line," eight English ships and eight French ships. They engaged in a two-hour battle. The French had the best of it with their longer-range cannon and eventually chased the British off. For four more days and nights, the two fleets engaged each other. A violent storm drove the French back inside the bay, and the English had to sail back to New York to repair their crippled fleet. One British ship was so badly damaged they had to blow it up. Back inside the bay, the French captured two British frigates. So, before Washington even arrived on the scene, Rochambeau had another 3,500 troops and siege cannon. Cornwallis's fate was sealed.

A Yorktown surrender was for all intents and purposes a foregone conclusion. At Yorktown, Cornwallis was only partly aware of the Capes' victory over the French. On September 29, Cornwallis received news the Clinton was sailing with another seven thousand troops in tow.

On the nights of October 6 and 7, American engineers dug trenches parallel to the British fortifications. The Americans began a second fortification on October 11 and 12. The allies lacked complete encirclement down to the river due to British redoubts placed there. On October 14, the French struck redoubt number 9, and Alexander Hamilton took redoubt number 10. The British tried to escape by crossing the river, but gale-force winds prevented the escape.

Cornwallis offered to surrender with honors of war, but Washington would only offer limited honors, having kept in mind Clinton's demand of complete surrender at Charleston. Cornwallis had no alternative but to accept. The British lost 156 dead, 326

wounded, and seventy missing. The Allies lost 113 dead and 258
wounded. The British surrendered 7,247 troops. The British garrison
marched out and had a choice of band music. They chose "A World
Turned Upside Down." The Revolutionary War was pretty much over.
Although it took more time to create a peace treaty, America had won
its independence from Britain.

FAITH

aith's next adventure came the next summer on her three-week vacation. She was to stay at an old plantation house that served as a British Army barracks until May 1882 when the British boarded their ships and sailed back to England with their tails between their legs, having just lost the Revolutionary War. A doctor/scientist lived next door. Dr. Germaine was famous for treating bacterial diseases with his own natural remedy. Faith met Dr. Germaine on a park bench, and they took an immediate liking to each other. She entertained him with her tops (dare call it research) and temperature change due to axial and orbital inclination changes and wobbles of the earth. She was fascinated with his work on viruses and bacterial disease. They decided to cooperate and formed a temporary partnership.

When she first looked into the microscope, she saw what looked like a lot of hairy little bugs and what looked like pebbles on a beach filling the rest of the glass plate. The viruses she was seeing were typhoid, typhus, diphtheria, syphilis, malaria, pneumonia, and gonorrhea. She carefully took the slide out from the microscope and put them in a sealed container and into the icebox. They identified the bacteria and classified them with their own names.

Dr. Germaine's flu medicine consisted of minerals, cilantro, mint, brussels sprouts, beans, bean leaves, bean sprouts, soda powder, baking soda, and hydrogen peroxide. They were encapsulated in beeswax. Dr. Germaine also took Faith out to Harlen Hills where there were some caves. He showed her how to scope up the gypsum on the edge of the cave. When they got back, he showed her how to mix the gypsum powder with water and use cotton cloth to make a cast that was good for broken arms and legs.

Faith and Dr. Germaine decide to take a walk by the park and came upon Larry Park. He invited them to sit with him on the bench and take a rest from walking. They found out he was staying in one of the old plantation slave houses next to the main plantation house that Faith was staying in. Larry had stayed loyal to the Patriots while the British soldiers stayed in the barracks in the main plantation house. Larry was on guard, and he gave the underground vital information about British deployment. They, in turn, gave the information to General Washington. It was only absolutely vital once. When General Washington needed to go south, first to Baltimore on his way to Yorktown, he needed a ruse to fool the British. He headed out just before midnight and had a small contingent of soldiers stay and keep the bonfires going. Larry assured the underground that the British had indeed taken the bait and General Henry Clinton had been completely fooled.

Faith told Larry that she would soon be going back to Baltimore. Larry warned Faith that there were many highway robbers on that route. He told her not to go by herself without armed bodyguards. She exclaimed that she, of course, had no bodyguards. Larry and Dr. Germaine volunteered to accompany her.

Faith, Dr. Germaine, and Larry hitched the wagon and headed out for Baltimore. They took the ferry across the Hudson and disembarked just south of Fort Lee. As they came close to Princetown, they came upon Marnie, her new baby, and her girlfriend, Christian. As they got about thirty miles past Princetown, they heard shots ring out.

About ten minutes later, another Negro Patriot came galloping up the road. He warned them that some robbers were right behind him. Larry and his new friend and Dr. Germaine stayed with the wagon and the baby. Larry had Marnie and Christian posted on the left side of the road, and about forty feet ahead of them, Faith was hidden on the right side of the road. They all had long rifles.

When the highway robbers approached, they were wearing masks and had pistols to hold up their victims. Larry ordered them to stop, holster their pistols, and dismount. He told them they were surrounded by armed men on both sides of the road. He told them to take off their masks and throw down their weapons. He then told them to remount, turn around, and head back to where they came from. He told them to pick up their gear and not stop until they reached Canada. He said one of his men was an artist and had no problem sketching their faces so they better not stop until they reached the border.

The group continued their journey to Baltimore. Larry and his newfound friend, Pete, decided to stay in Baltimore and work in the Stevens warehouse. Dr. Germaine and his long rifle—along with his new pistols given up by the highway robbers—loaded up his wagon with duty-free food and supplies, thanks to Stevens, and headed back to Manhattan. Marnie, her baby, and Christian were met by Johann, her husband, and Michael and David in a new partnership farm. They provided plenty of protection in case highway robbers were on the loose.

Faith settled back into her new accounting work, and all the others, including Larry and Pete, commenced working in the Stevens docks, warehouses, and customshouse. Paul Stevens made his way to Germantown, Pennsylvania, and joined General Washington's army. He fought in the Germantown Battle east and north of the city and joined the forces to go to winter quarters at Valley Forge. The winter was bitter cold, and the soldiers were unclothed, unfed, and without firewood. Paul decided to desert and crawled out of camp to find food and clothing. He was found sitting against a tree with blood on his feet. In the early spring, Paul Stevens was tried and convicted of desertion and ordered executed. Washington gathered all his troops. The deserters were mounted on horses and had lynching rope tied around their necks. Washington lowered his sword, the horses bolted, and the deserters were hung with broken necks.

MARNIE

Marnie and her mother stayed in Philadelphia for the rest of the war. They reoccupied the house the British had used for its soldiers. As they suspected, it was occupied by rank-and-file soldiers who would have been their clients in prostitution. Marnie got her two jobs back as a schoolteacher and a librarian. She also took an interest in a Franklin printing press shop and got an apprenticeship there. She liked that work even though it was a bit tedious.

Marnie's mother, Charlotte, had her kitting and needlework, and she also found work in a coffee shop. They were set up well with Joann's father's retirement, but they still liked to keep busy. They both enjoyed working and the company it provided.

Charlotte said, "I wonder if James will ever come around again."

Marnie replied, "Well, if he doesn't, we'll get along with our lives just fine." "He will probably hold it against me if he does come around since he thinks I sabotaged him as far as you were concerned."

'He'll get over it. After all, we didn't owe him anything. It's not as if you owed him a pledge of my affections."

"We're both independent women now, and we'll get along just fine without men in our lives."

"I like my two jobs and my apprenticeship, and I'm thinking about writing a book called *Daniel Morgan's Time*, which will be all about our time with General Morgan, including elsewhere in the world and the past, present, and future perspective of our history." "That would be nice. You could also include Philip Brady's travels."

"Yes, he'll have a lot of stories to tell about all the countries he's been to and his two marriages."

While James was serving, he took part in the battle at Camden. Camden was an unmitigated disaster! Although their forces were evenly matched, the British clearly routed the hapless (and leaderless) Americans. However, James did himself proud by killing a few British soldiers and officers.

Gates had fled the scene at the first sight of the British presence and made his way across the entire state of North Carolina and halfway through Virginia before he stopped to give his horses a rest. James was rewarded for this cowardice by being assigned to General Morgan's militia. Morgan was recommissioned by George Washington and Nathanael Greene and made a general on Nathanael Greene's southern army. Morgan mistakenly wanted to restore Gates's reputation as a loyal soldier, but Gates deserved little loyalty or acclaim. The Continental Congress did as Washington recommended and made Gates an adjunct general in charge of requisitioning food and supplies for Washington's army.

James made himself proud and served well under General Morgan at Cowpens and under Nathanael Greene at Guilford Courthouse. He stayed with General Greene through North Carolina, South Carolina, and all the way to Charleston, surrounding the British until the end of the war.

James was still hurting when he arrived back in Philadelphia, and although he didn't hold a grudge against Joann, he hated her mother. After he settled back on his farm, he learned Joann had stayed in Philadelphia and was once again a librarian and an elementary teacher. He heard that Joann's father had helped her annul her marriage to the

British officer, but he didn't know the details. Believing he had lost out, he dedicated himself to the farm life. Through Joann, James heard the good news that Philip had arrived back in New York and had his new family with him.

When Philip arrived back in Philadelphia, his old friend was extremely distraught and depressed. James told him how Marnie's mother had conspired against him in convincing Marnie to marry that blaggard British officer. He was pretty much inconsolable. Philip worked on him for days and finally convinced him to at least visit Marnie and learn of her plight.

The four old friends—Philip, Joann, Marnie, and James—finally met up. James asked Marnie why she had stooped to such a low as to marry an enemy soldier and why, for God's sake, she would listen to her conspiratorial mother. Marnie explained that they were in danger of being made prostitutes for the British regulars if they didn't find a way out. She said she had no idea her husband-to-be was homosexual. Philip, Joann, and James had never heard the word before, and Marnie was too embarrassed to tell them. When they looked up the word, they were speechless.

Although James still blamed Marnie's mother for her mishaps, he still asked her to marry him. She was elated at his proposal since it was what she wanted all along. Their marriage was attended by a large gathering of friends and family, including Joann, Christine, and baby Tiffany. Philip and his new bride and family were there. Their friends from Baltimore—Albert, Bell, Thomas, Virginia and Opra—were there too. Philip's family and the James family were there. Joann's parents were there too. There was a congregation of around one hundred people. James and his new bride decided to take a long honeymoon and went to Niagara Falls. James counted himself as the luckiest man on earth!

FAITH

Faith's work was about to pay off in telling the Stevens that they would either have to sell their plantation and slaves or sell them and buy a customhouse and warehouse. Mr. Stevens decided to sell the plantation, free his slaves, and buy the Customhouse and the Warehouse Then he moved his family and friends to Baltimore where his new purchases were located. All of the freed Slaves decided to stay with Mr. Stevens and work for him for fair wages.

Faith stayed with the Stevens and was now in charge of the accounting and double entry bookkeeping of the customhouse and the warehouse. She promptly put them both in good financial standing and made them a growing enterprise. She advised Mr. Stevens to accept both Continental currency as well as British Pound Sterling.

The accounting office was located behind the customhouse near a swamp. Faith often went out to lunch near the swamp when she thought the mosquitoes were flying toward the nearby livestock. Unbeknownst to her, they could smell her blood—and she was savagely bitten by them. After all, her family was there. The Stevens family was there. Thomas and his wife were there. She slowly slipped away during the night. Faith felt really sick and went home. The wailing, grieving, and sorrow that took place after that were unbelievable.

It was a very solemn occasion. Faith's funeral procession included her Grandma Opra, her pallbearers, her grieving family, her fellow workers, and her dear friends. The Stevens family followed with her other white friends and coworkers. It was quite unusual for a procession to have Negroes followed by whites instead of the reverse. The grief and sense of loss were felt by all.

Faith's grieving Pappa blamed her loss on the devil. He felt like the devil had possessed Faith's top, her drawings, and her data sheets. He confessed to Thomas that he had been very jealous about Thomas being with his wife so much of the time at the plantation. Thomas told him he was really surprised by that and loved him, Albert, Bell, and Faith. They were like family to him. Albert apologized for his indiscretion.

"You too, dear Thomas, are family to us. You were as good as Faith's uncle and a brother for me and Bell."

Thomas convinced Albert to put Faith's work in a trunk and save it for posterity. "God save us, Thomas, and Faith is most assuredly at the right hand of the Lord. God bless you, dear, loving, and generous daughter who most people could only dream of."

THOMAS'S MILITARY PARADE

Thomas and the Negro troops were to go on parade before Alexander Hamilton, the secretary of the Treasury, and John Adams, the vice president, in Baltimore. The white troops went first and had an abysmal showing. They were in disorder as they marched, their uniforms were tawdry and unkempt, and when they stood to fire a parade volley, their shots went off in such disorder that they thoroughly embarrassed themselves. In contrast, the Negro unit was organized with their marching, their progression movements, and their manual of arms. Their uniforms and boots were spiffy and polished. At the end of their manual of arms, their musket volleys sounded as one.

"It's amazing," Hamilton said. "The pride and professionalism of the Negro troops, and since the war is over, the whites just don't seem to give a damn."

Adams said, "You would think we would have destroyed their spirit by now, but we've been proven wrong."

They were extremely impressed with the Negro soldiers and sent congratulations to the commander and his men.

MICHAEL AND DAVID

S hortly after Marnie and James got back from their wilderness honeymoon in Niagara Falls, Marnie got a very strange letter from England. It was from Michael's. They hadn't heard from him, and some other parents hadn't heard from his friend David either. They suspected that they had deserted shortly after the British occupation of Philadelphia. They wondered whether Marnie had heard of their whereabouts. Marnie was taken aback by this, but she could see she'd need help finding them.

She asked Joann if her father could get his detective from Morristown to help find them. Detective Summers had some vacation time coming, and he said he could work on it for a few days.

Detective Summers rode out to Philadelphia and began to scour the state records regarding land purchases. He soon found that these two men had bought land in western Pennsylvania, not far from where Marnie and James lived.

Marnie was delighted that she could help reunite Michael and David with their parents. Since the war was over, there was no real danger to the men. James, however, was very pensive. After all, he considered Michael to be his nemesis! He calmed down, and they took a wagon to meet the two ex-officers.

The two were pleased to find out that Marnie could send a letter to England without arousing suspicion from the British military. Although the war was over, they still didn't feel safe yet. Marnie promptly sent them a letter and the parents of both boys decided to come and join them in America where people weren't "subjects."

MORGAN

Daniel Morgan led the offensive and positioned the defensive first strike in Saratoga. His aggressive nature was intended to give the enemy no choice but to flee. He kept up the pressure as the enemy fled for cover and again as they retreated to their final position. This pressure had to shorten the battle and pin down the enemy for an easy surrender under overwhelming odds. Pressing the battle took away any chance to escape and regroup. They had the forts and the waterways, but pressing the battle basically cut them off from any kind of retreat.

Morgan was responsible for both the strategic and tactical plan for Cowpens. He chose the ground and engineered his fighting strategy by placing the militia in front of the regulars so they could run and reload. It resulted in a complete double envelopment, which had not been seen since Hannibal conquered the Romans by bringing elephants across the Alps to outflank the Romans. It was also a complete route that wiped out Cornwallis's cavalry. It was the turning point of the war in the South.

Morgan was able to take the prisoners to Virginia before the rivers became unnavigable. The water was rising. Nathanael Greene was in a position to put up a defensive position, but the British were for all intents and purposes retreating from North Carolina and eventually surrendering. Nathanael Greene emulated Morgan's tactics at Guilford Courthouse, but he lost some aggression at a turning point in the battle and had to retreat.

Cornwallis was retreating from North Carolina altogether and had a diminished army to show for it. His actions in the South had been completely superfluous. Morgan was the decisive action that led to two major British surrenders in the northern and the southern theaters. He was at the turning point in both the northern theater and the southern theater. His participation may have been second only to Washington in winning the war. He was probably the best all-around commander in both armies in both strategy and tactics.

How the British Could
Have Won the War

It's really a very simple proposition. If the British had contented themselves to occupying the major cities, they could have waited out the Whigs. Instead, they trampled around the countryside, never controlling more than the piece of earth they currently occupied. They could have—after taking New York and staying in Philadelphia, Charleston, and Savannah—proceeded to then-occupied Baltimore and then marched to Boston from Newport, occupying the city and its outskirts. They then could have waited out the Americans and either given amnesty to the likes of Benjamin Franklin, George Washington, and Thomas Jefferson or put them in a guerilla contest where they probably would have been starved into submission.

Happy Families

In *Anna Karenina*, Leo Tolstoy wrote, "Happy families are all the same, but unhappy families are all unique each in its own way." Marnie and James and their parents, Joann, Christine, Tiffany and their parents, Philip, Nadia, Olga, Vladimer, Virginia and Thomas, Bell, Albert, and Opra, and Michael and David and their parents had all bought farms and settled in western Pennsylvania. They were celebrating their good fortune by having dinner at the home of Marnie and James.

It was late November, and the crops had been harvested. They were having turkey, yams, baked potatoes, corn, baked beans, corn bread, and pumpkin and apple pie with whipped cream. Marnie started a champagne toast by happily but tearfully announcing, "James and I are proud to announce that I am with child and God willing will deliver the dear one in the late spring or early summer. Hear, hear!"

Philip asked to toast to his new family.

Michael and David's parents asked for a toast to Michael and David's new partnership. Last but not least, Thomas said, "Could we all toast to the beautiful, gifted genius—our dear Faith. Albert assured me my niece is at the right hand of the Lord."

"God loves you, and God blesses you, our beloved Faith," they all said in chorus. "So, let us say grace," offered James. "Bless us, O Lord, for these thy gifts, which we are about to receive from thy bounty through Christ our Savior. Amen."

So, it may be true that all happy families are the same, but this one was especially blessed.

In her brilliance she fairly represents all that her people could have accomplished if not for the yoke of the Great White Devil!

FAITH'S LEGACY

Cary had her new girlfriend, Casey, with her and was very happy. She had met her in rehab, and it was love at first sight. Early also had his girlfriend with him. Her name was Lately. Early was not an addictive personality, but he knew he was obsessive-compulsive and an enabler. He attended rehab with Cary to lend his support. He had recently taken up needlework and had made many pieces of fine art. Drapey started writing historical fiction. Dooty was busy with her calculus, as always, but she had also taken up astrophysics. Although she was not an addictive personality, Gaugy decided to attend rehab with Cary to lend her support as well. She was a yoga instructor and modern dancer.

Dooty requested and received the trunk that Faith's father and her avuncular uncle had stored her work in. She opened it and found a nice surprise: Faith's drawings and data related to her top work. Faith had recognized that when the top wobbled off of its axis, it reproduced what Milankovitch recognized as apsidal and perihelion precession. Faith also saw that the orbit of the top changed as it wobbled. This was what Milankovitch recognized as *obliquity*. Faith also saw that the top eventually wobbled into an expanded ellipse. She recognized—as did Milankovitch—that it was eccentricity.

Although Faith's father was unable to see the beauty of Faith's work, her uncle had persuaded him to preserve the work.

"For where your treasure is, there your heart will be also" (Matthew 6:21).

BIBLIOGRAPHY

1.) The Compact History of the Revolutionary War (Compact Histories Book 1) by R. Ernest Dupuy (Author), Trevor N. Dupuy (Author)
2.) Paul Revere's Ride by David Hackett Fischer
3.) The First Salute : A View of the American Revolution by Barbara W. Tuchman
4.) The Murder of Napoleon Paperback – February 17, 1999 by David Hapgood (Author) This book investigates the case made by Swedish Dentist Dr. Sten Forshufvud.
5.) Encyclopedia Britanica
6.) Wikipedia.com

Printed in the United States
by Baker & Taylor Publisher Services